Joseph Turnley

The king

The First Plantagenet

Joseph Turnley

The king
The First Plantagenet

ISBN/EAN: 9783337342319

Printed in Europe, USA, Canada, Australia, Japan

Cover: Foto ©Andreas Hilbeck / pixelio.de

More available books at **www.hansebooks.com**

THE KING;

OR,

THE FIRST PLANTAGENET.

A Drama.

DEDICATED TO SIR SALAR JUNG,

ON THE OCCASION OF

His Visit to England.

By JOSEPH TURNLEY.

AUTHOR OF "THE LIFE AND TIMES OF RICHARD CŒUR DE LION,"
"THE LANGUAGE OF THE EYE,"
"ROYAL REVERIES ON IMMORTALITY," ETC., ETC.

WITH ILLUSTRATIONS BY SIR JOHN GILBERT, A.R.A.

London:
A. H. BAILY AND CO., CORNHILL.

1876.

Dedication.

In dedicating this drama—THE KING—to *Sir Salar Jung*, I venture to observe that the presence of this faithful subject of the "Empress of India," is an event of the greatest interest to Englishmen, and cannot fail to evince to the youths of this country that such glory, beauty, and refinement as the life and conduct of this valiant man has displayed cannot fail to attract the notice and admiration of the great and good, and that neither distance nor time can eclipse the light of a great soul. In Sir Salar Jung heroism itself seems gracefully ennobled and magnificently enshrined.

We may perhaps partly trace this visit to that timely and wise undertaking, namely, the journey to India of our gallant Prince, His Royal Highness the Prince of Wales, and the invitation of the courteous and much-respected nobleman, His Grace the Duke of Sutherland. Queen Victoria does not possess a more faithful and useful subject than Sir Salar Jung of Hyderabad.

There have been many conquerors who returning from fields of blood have won the praise and gratitude of England's princes and people, and have received liberal rewards. We might instance Marlborough, Wellington, and others.

Such conquerors have mostly been inducted to and living in the very grooves of war, surrounded by every concomitant aid and appliance, supplemented by a waiting anxious nation, and watched by able and critical officials.

Dedication.

In Sir Salar Jung we recognize the highest class of conqueror, standing almost alone, and far distant from supreme
government. This hero triumphed without spilling a single
drop of human blood, whilst commanding and teaching tens of
thousands of his countrymen that rebellion to England was the
sure way to disgrace, ignominy, and death. He turned the
current of events.

Yes, it was by his astounding influence (nurtured by a long
period of noble acts and pure government) that he at the very
risk of his life prevented the alienation of Southern India, and
a scene of blood-sheddings and rebellion which no pen can
describe. Alone he unfurled the defiant flag of old England
amidst tens of thousands who were alone bayed by his courage
and wisdom !

If this is true,—and where is the Englishman who will deny
it ?—then let England *en masse* wish and pray that health, hap_
piness, and success may attend our distinguished visitor, and
that if England possesses any tribute good enough and especially suitable for his acceptance it may (whatever it may be)
be presented without delay or deduction.

June, 1876.

THE AUTHOR'S PREFACE.

—◆—

To say why a great man appears on the stage of this world at a particular epoch, or what of his own individual genius he imparts to the generation in which he appears, is beyond our power; but the fact is certain, that society is ever and anon resuscitated by the presence of such spirits, to whom the debilitated immobility and succumbing state of the governed, and the warring tyranny of the civil or ecclesiastical government, are revolting and almost intolerable. It is then, under the influence of an intellectual and heartfelt anguish, they determine to summon all their powers to satisfy their unconquerable desire to restore order, and animate many powers waiting for a leader to create permanent establishments for the growth and preservation of liberty and justice.

For awhile they astound and illuminate (in the midst of some errors and weaknesses too subtle to be foreseen), yet they pause not whilst performing feats of grandeur and glory which give to humanity new, exalting, and salutary influences. They remain awhile to perform their mission, and though time carries away their mortality (as the day star in the western seas), yet their works live after them, to illumine and embrighten future cycles of time. Such a character these pages (though imperfectly) are intended to portray.

"The First Plantagenet" may be regarded as part of that brilliant militant host who, travelling in their greatness, have stamped upon the rigidity of many obstacles which might have delayed the triumph of liberty.

The dramatic form has been selected as likely to impress on the mind some of those interesting and remarkable qualities, with which spirits (though unseen) were ever inciting this heroic being. Each day of his eventful life he seemed to come forth clad in some fresh fervour and grand impulse he had been taught in mystic reveries.

It may be true that history and biography should abound with facts, material and obvious, such as wars and great acts of governments; yet there are moral, hidden facts, veiled for a time, which are no less real than the unseen parts of physical man. Indeed, they may be regarded as more essentially operative than the more palpable and obvious.

It is hoped the reader will not assume any of the sentiments in this volume as pointed at any existing ecclesiastical establishment.

The chief characters are *pari passu* with Lord Littleton's life of the Second Henry. It is believed the assassination of À Becket was not dictated by the king. The Duchess de Bretagne, and some subordinates, may be regarded as types of the characters moving around the royal person.

January, 1876.

Dramatis Personæ.

———◆———

THE KING, HENRY II.

GEOFFERY, *the* KING'S *natural Son.*

À BECKET, *Archbishop of Canterbury.*

BISHOP *of* CHICHESTER.

RICHARD DE LUCEY, *Chief Justice.*

RANDOLPH DE GLANVILLE.

WALTER MAPES.

PETER OF BLOIS.

ELEANOR, QUEEN *of* HENRY II.

DUCHESS DE BRETAGNE.

ROSAMOND DE CLIFFORD, *Mistress of the* KING.

Priests, Courtiers, Servants, *and others.*

INTRODUCTION.

THESE pages are respectfully presented to the public as a record of some parts of the life of one of England's most noble, heroic, and politic kings, whose resistance of priestly arrogance and aggression in the twelfth century led to reformations of no ordinary character. Henry II., the first Plantagenet, was ever willing to recognize the Church as the natural ally of the State, and never its slave ; but he demanded that it should always be its voluntary subject. He acknowledged the Church had innate dignity, and that it commanded the attention of the reflecting philosopher and active politician. That she was the natural arbiter and keeper of many things which advance the peace and order of man and the comfort and taste of society. That while some systems were but imperfect imitative theories, wanting power and state, the genius of her hierarchy was exact, extensive, and well delineated.

The Church was announced as the bride of Divinity, clad in its robes and decked with its graces. Her high-born lineage awakened many lofty assumptions ; and though her foot was on the earth, yet she quivered not, whilst she marshalled all her properties with an energetic movement and order, wholly irresistible by all worldly dynasties. She once wore a grace and auspiciousness, which the conventions reared by the magi of this world never possessed. The divine character she had assumed, united to the sublime purpose she declared, commanded for her an imperial position, an extensive dominion, and a grandeur of state which secured the reverence of millions. Her very vocation rendered her a leader and a dictator ; for she professed one vast and immeasurable end, viz., to arouse the millions of spirits of men to a sense of their own dignity and power. Mighty and extraordinary are her functions ever assumed by her priests for placing before man the secrets of his own nature, with its degree of individual power and honour attainable in this world, and laying before him the jewels of the treasury of heaven.

But let her cease to expose her dignity, grace, and power by vain exhibitions and haughty assumptions, which delay the union of the Churches and the development of liberty.

The Church should be the source of all the peace and happiness which ever elevated man's nature and enlivened man's earthly path, containing within its bosom light and loveliness, which neither man, nor fiend, nor time, nor eternity can ever put out. She was the keeper of the pandects of eternity. Many were the graces of love and charity which distinguished her from all other conventions. The light of knowledge glowed upon her brow, and, associating with her divine pretensions, secured for her real grandeur and power. She was conservator of the arts and sciences, of vast knowledge, and all those elegant attainments which should regulate and refine society. It was in the twelfth century the Church assumed new characteristics, by the influence of the Pope, who induced the first Henry to admit his Legate into England.

Yet even in the early part of the first Plantagenet's reign, the Church (notwithstanding its incomparable acumen) had scarcely ascertained the nature of its powers, or the most effective mode of using them. Its thirst for self-aggrandizement did not blind its acute eye, which perceived that there revolved in the spirit of the English monarch many sublime principles, which were not easily bent to subjection. Quickly indeed was England, with its monarch and all its glorious and ingenuous properties, weighed in the balances of the Vatican ; but the whole Papal council could not immediately determine whether the king of England was better suited for an ally or a victim of the hierarchy. Many were the vacillations and hesitations of the Church, in which it may be compared to a young vulture, who could just espy her prey flickering below the craggy height, where misfortune or circumstance had cast it ; but who dared not pounce upon it with that eagerness her carnivorous nature dictated, lest her half-fledged wing should fail, or her intended victim overmatch her strength.

In the twelfth century the power of the Church was by no means comprehended. The sovereigns of Europe, and England in particular, suddenly saw a monstrous thing stalking forth upon the earth, with the mien and comeliness of an angel ; but they knew not that its designs were subversive of the power and happiness of man. Its ends and purposes were impervious to the common ken, but its aim was power unprecedented. It sought to be regarded as the Deity ruling on earth. For a time, kings and princes and warlike men fell back; and like frighted steeds, with distended nostrils and ears erect, snorting and champing, yet looking intently on some strange object, they paused to gaze at what they could not understand. For awhile their eyes were riveted upon it; yet they soon returned to their respective vocations, for they felt incompetent to contend with a being that they thought belonged to the powers of heaven or hell. In other words, a new principle had come to herd with the corruptions of the earth. Its nature was too sublime and active to rank under any common vassalage; indeed, the monarchs of the earth already displayed both jealousy and deference, for they believed it had within its grasp some vast treasury and mystic panoply, which was as unfathomable as it was august, and sufficient to render it either a valuable ally or a dangerous enemy. The lusts of time and power were soon detected as an eminent part of its nature.

The ways and doings of the Church rendered the chief government debilitated and timid, and the constitution seemed tottering. It was at this crisis that Providence raised up the noble and generous monarch Henry II., who required not the authority of ancestral rights nor the aid of long-settled institutions; for his genius was so elevated and independent, that its action aggrandized its owner to the highest degree of magnificence and dignity. In its career there was a glory about it so conspicuous and transcendent, that whilst the noble and great felt it honourable to be allied to it, the vicious shrank before its development. His predecessors had been satisfied with the title of king, and gratified with their limited territories in France, and were content to be "lord of lords;" but he had determined to hold England in one hand and France in the other, and plant his standard in lands almost unknown to his predecessors, and (if we may be allowed the expression) bearing the inscription, "King of kings." He was the sun and shield of all. Yes; he was the soul of his people; and through him every hope, every wish, and every fear passed ere it could have practical character. His public conduct secured for him the highest dignity of monarchy, viz., Chief Conservator of Public Peace. He seemed endued with the vital organs just adapted to the imperial and massive genius of monarchy.

As king, warrior, and statesman, Henry II. had no equal; he was far above and beyond the day in which he lived. Even his private character was the display of superiority which a refined and elegant mind was ever striving to hide — it was

b

seductive and interesting. Such was the dignity of the prince whose resistance of priestly presumption awakened in some degree the glorious Reformation, but whose spirit, because ambitious, earthy, and glory-seeking, was ultimately overwhelmed by the intrigues of the Vatican. There is no scandal in saying there ever was an inherent enmity in Popery towards civil monarchy, and that it has been the policy of the Popes ·to endeavour to hide this predisposition from the observation of the monarchs of Europe, except when the Papal power became irresistible. This demand of supremacy, this hostility to civil monarchs, is not a mere incident, but belongs to the very existence and nature of Roman Catholicism, and to every dynasty which pretends to a supremacy over the conscience and soul of man.

The appointment of À Becket to the see of Canterbury increased the presumption of the Church. Indeed, it gave birth to a sudden, protracted, and irritating animosity between the Church and the King of England. In this À Becket took the foremost part.

In Henry's reign Romanism affected but a formalism ; yet it soon claimed to be the dictator, not only in religious matters, but in many important civil matters, and, like all usurpers, became bold and cruel in effecting every end its pride desired. Its great assumption was that of a complete vicegerency of Heaven to rule the acts and rights of all men — to govern all thought, morals, opinions, and conscience. It was under the protection of such unbounded power that it oft perpetrated with impunity, perjury, murder, incest, blasphemy, and crimes of the worst description.

Such was the dark state of the world, that all conventions, more or less, were suppliantly bowing before the ecclesiastical dynasty ; and the mass oft-times threw themselves, in the most humiliating form, before this Juggernaut of Paganism. To resist this leviathan, or check its progress, even for a time, became the task or privilege of a mind which could see beyond and out of the darkness around. It was not only necessary to awaken, but to guide a sufficient means for the end, and to divert, if possible, all the vast and valuable capacities of the Church to their proper vocation. For this it required all the reason of a superior mind, with unprecedented physical powers; but even these would ever have been insufficient for the great engagement, unless they had been upheld by the highest degree of station and authority, and free, in a great measure, from that passion and weakness which too generally mingle in man. It required a being, or rather a spirit, which could set up a standard of ethics and moral right, with an individual independence unaffected by the dark delusions around. It required a passionate and barbarian love for liberty, united to a civilized genius and acumen. The true sentiment of human spontaneity in its most vigorous and unrestricted development, the love of nature and of man, the defiance of archives and pandects, and all which had been and might be. ' It required that noble sensitiveness, yet headstrong resolution, which seems truly derivative from high moral nature. It is rather difficult for us, in regulated society, to comprehend the vastness and magnificence of the spirit which must have urged the first Plantagenet in many of his extraordinary feats. Such men have been, and have stepped this earthly arena for awhile ; but the rapid advance of civilization seems to have destroyed the chief features of their grand development.

This great prince sought to establish moral influence, and the moderate separation of temporal and spiritual power; for, in their confusion, he saw the many vicious principles which have ever had so baneful an effect on the progress of civilization. This great task required a resolution, which neither the threats of the mighty could shake, nor the indifference of the superior class, nor the torpor of the unnumbered multitude, could distract from its great vocation. For it was a war of years, pointed against the prejudices of a mighty class which no man could number—against the partialities of nations of warriors and philosophers, and against the alliances and affections of many of the kings and potentates of the earth. The treasures of the world, the might of physical action, the patronage of honours and riches—the gifts of the present, and the promises and hopes of the future world—were in possession of the great enemy that was now to be attacked. This enemy had held a fortress impregnable for generations, whose towers once touched heaven, and whose foundations were now blanched with the bones of thousands who had presumed to doubt its perfection, or to attempt to reduce its arrogance. But it now perceived that one of the champions of the human family, yet in his youth, in manhood's gallant hour, for awhile with less earthly weakness, had thrown off the shackles which the human interpreters of the Divine will had attempted to cast upon him, and was not afraid to measure lances with the leaders of the ecclesiastical government.

It was then that the defensive life and faculty which reigned within their mystic arcana were first tried and contended with. There was then a sudden exercise of all that was splendid, mighty,

and cruel. It was then that the degree of criminality and un-
faithfulness to which the tyranny of the Papacy could dare to
extend itself, was added to the miscellaneous band of its powers.
It was then that the meanest of the monastic order was invited
to cast all his tiny share of cloistered cunning and pelf into the
gathering tide of the common cause ; which, fed by ten thousand
tributary streams, did, by the vastness of its aggregate, astonish
both friend and antagonist. It was then that the coffers of the
Church, which had been filling during a long period of darkness,
were opened and emptied forth, with a haste and zeal that
afforded but little opportunity of distinguishing the tribute of
blood from the gold which common intimidation and promises
had ground from generations, in other lands, long since hidden
in their graves. It was then that the less differences between
the superior and inferior ecclesiastics were willingly laid aside,
and for awhile forgotten ; whilst every energy was put forth
against the spirit which threatened to expose the human nature
and imperfection of that convention, which had been so long
revered as altogether divine and immaculate. Yes ! it was then
that national councils, provincial councils, general councils, with
their perpetual correspondence and publication of letters and of
admonitions, carefully exercised their functions to one common
end. Not for the search of any great truth was the intellectual
life which resided in the bosom of this government then used,
but for the preservation of principles vicious and destructive !
For it was then that the Church discovered that there still
resided within the temporal power that brute physical force (the
only resuscitating means), which, if guided by a just and noble
arm, would realize a government superior and more worthy of
love than the ecclesiastical system was willing to provide. The
Papacy had for some time felt, that as long as the temporal ruler
was satisfied to receive a part of the plunder which its various
agents had from time to time torn from the people, without in-
vestigating the degree and nature of the violence employed,
there was still hope that the temporal power might be kept in
subjection, and regarded as the inferior power. It was when
the civil government suddenly hesitated to lend to the Church
its physical powers of punishment, and claimed for itself an
individuality of character and action, that the ecclesiastical
monarchy proved that its own mystic machinery (however secret,
demoniac, and cruel), which gleamed through interstices of the
hierarchical fabric, was insufficient alone to keep at bay that
spirit which had been provoked to wrestle in the gloom of moral
darkness. For this spirit feared, that while the Church was

recklessly tearing off the remaining features of that moral beauty and independence which its Maker had mantled it with, an arm was raised to destroy all the good order and public tranquillity of all the regular jurisdiction of the laws and of the king's sovereignty itself, and, by sure consequence, of the whole state.

The martial character of Henry did not destroy his love of society. He married the accomplished Eleonora when she had just attained her thirty-first year, whilst he was in his twenty-first year; but this contract did not stay or interrupt the development of his leading dispositions. At an early period of the career of Henry II., ambition taught him to regard all danger and fatigues as the flowers which were indigenous in the path to glory and dominion, in which he must make many sacrifices.

But a few days after his marriage with the fascinating Eleonora, he left her insinuating loveliness to seek the face of his enemies. It might be said of him that, when he knew he required sleep, he only took that rest which restored his body to its perfect powers; but he never slumbered or folded his arms. Everything that sustained the comfort of his people or the honour of royalty was now under his own eye; indeed, the good order of cities, the improvement of agriculture, manufactures, and trade, occupied a just portion of the mind of this mighty and chivalrous being. He was a king; he claimed not to be a delegate of Heaven, or heir to all earthly sovereignty; but he bowed to listen to the sighs and wishes of a misgoverned and noble people; and thus, by duly respecting their comforts and his own dignity, he formed the model of a monarchy which was destined to generate principles that have formed a part of the present peace and happiness of England.

That he might be temperate and energetic at all times, he knew that he must keep his body under, and ofttimes exercised a self-denial both in eating and drinking, which astonished his courtiers. In his dress he regarded all ornament as an incumbrance and an effeminate association, which might in the hour of strife or danger become a hindrance. This is too often disregarded from its minuteness or fascination, but has in some signal instances given that little balance of advantage to an antagonist, which has turned, in the person of the leader, the scale of fortune against nations long revered for their municipal wisdom and warlike power. Yet it must not be assumed that he was ignorant or regardless how much the mass, the herding multitude, are affected by splendid equipage and gorgeous display; but he ruled them by superior and more majestic powers. He was not unaware that the soft eye of woman delighted to

bend over brilliant dress and elegant ornament; but his manly
and dignified person, his expressive and serene eyes, soon pro-
cured a preference in woman's heart, for one whose knightly fortune and warlike successes had become as the living romance
of those romantic times.

The history of his gallantries seems rather impervious and
indistinct, and some historians have said they throw a shadow
on his character, and that the love of woman produced many
enemies and detracting factions. Although the softer passions,
such as love, may give fervour and energy to many of the act-
ions of life, and without them our nature seems gloomy and
uninteresting; yet this great king most frequently governed
them as servitors, to bow under the dark and lofty banner
of ambition. He well knew that to become the too docile
subject of sensual appetites was to disturb the great attributes
of the mind from their inherent action, and to destroy the
powers of that body which should be a companion to the spirit
in all its earthly exaltations. Therefore neither Rosamond the
Fair, nor the handsome Stafford maiden, nor all that is lovely
in woman or flattering in man, seemed likely to seduce the
mind of Henry from the great vocation of ambition and the
leading objects of his life.

In tracing, however slightly, this energetic being, Henry II.,
from the buoyant age of eighteen, and through the various
vicissitudes and deep anxieties which ever attended his path,
we shall observe that most of such trials and struggles seemed
rather to develop the powers and resources of his mind, than
to crush or overwhelm him : some were light as playful bubbles,
bursting on the face of the current; some as billows soon joined
the general stream. But there was one as a wild tide, producing
angry eddies and dinning whirlpools, which have ever and anon
threatened to dash the noble swimmer to the depths of ruin.
Or, if we may presume to alter the simile, Henry II. and his
Primate (an ecclesiastic of vast talent, learning, and martial
courage) were as two mighty tides, seen by the timid traveller
in the trackless seas, contending with each other, so that their
chief powers were spent in breaking each other's form and
comeliness. It is difficult to conceive what would have been
the result of Henry's reign, if À Becket had never been en-
trusted with the see of Canterbury; but it is very probable that
some most useful and important reforms were prevented by this
circumstance.

The king's successes in war were most remarkable, and much
aided his imperial position; indeed, he became the subject of

universal love and admiration. The strategy of Rome, united to the conspiracy of his Queen and sons, led to that great change which attend on all human fortune.

Henry II. as a conqueror, surrounded by the brave and triumphant, was a dazzling spectacle ; but when the storm of life set in, and with pelting violence followed him everywhere, his hardy frame at last yielded and sank. The shock must have been tremendous to a spirit wholly unschooled to humiliation. Alas ! what can describe the intense agony that quivered through the mortal frame tenanted by this undaunted spirit, when the dream of his invincibleness was broken, and the tide of his victories rolled back, with the shock of his destruction echoing through all Europe ! That immeasurable weight of horror, which then entered this spirit, could find no place on earth to bear it up ; but heaving headlong in his mortal parts, urged them down even to the relentless grave. A violent fever attacking him on the 6th day of July, 1189, at the city of Chinon, he caused himself to be carried into the church, before the altar, supported by the arms of Geoffery, the youngest son of Rosamond ; where, heaving several heavy sighs, and throwing his head on the bosom of Geoffery, he gave up the ghost. His reign was amongst the longest of England's princes, viz., thirty-four years, eight months, and twelve days. Stebbing, in his "Kings of England," says, Henry's burial was thus :—" Clothede in royal robes, crown on his head, white gloves on his hands, boots of gold upon his legs, gilt spurs on his heels, a great rich ring upon his finger, his sceptre in his hand, his sword by his side, and his face all bare and uncovered."

But hark ! we hear the shouts of war ; the neighing of fiery chargers ; and the blood-stained garment floats on the breeze. The mountains hear the voice of woe. Cries are heard in the valleys, and the mighty rivers are swollen with blood. Beside the limpid water, and by the golden sand, Christian and Moor lie blanching in the wind. But see ! there comes one mightier than the rest, with hues as varied as the bow of heaven. As some tall pine, he tops the myriads round ; his sable plumes wave like terrific clouds ; his vest is smeared with gore ; his clanking mail resounds as the troubled waters of Acheron. 'Tween heaven and earth, like a dark fiend, he comes ; his eyes flash with fire and rage ; midst groves of spears he cleaves his fearful way, fierce as an angry boar. His charger is as the charger of Death ; she paws the yielding air, and tramples on the slain, the brave, the gory, tired brave (where stained and broken

armour, and foaming steeds and dying men, in one vast ruin lie).
His lance is like some weaver's beam ; his ponderous axe smokes
with bright blood ; it seems as though the Judgment Day were
come, and yet he smiles and rallies thousands to his floating
banner.   He smiles, as if in summer sport, to see the thousands
entering the first morn of the eternal world ; they are his fellows,
the equals of this king.   He joys with Death—gaunt Death—to
see the share he takes ; and Death taunts and grins again. A shrill
and piercing cry comes o'er the blasted heath, and all is still.
The herald's vaunting trumpet sounds— " Richard, the warrior
king, the prince of chivalry, Richard, Cœur de Lion, knight of
the Holy Wars ! "

And now another king appears.
The moral purpose of this elevated personage is to watch the
development and action of society with a pure zeal and unceas-
ing superintendence, so as to secure by majestic authority the
greatest possible degree of happiness to that part of the human
family who obey his nod and maintain the grandeur and circumstance of the daily revelation of his office. This is the purpose
of England's Queen, Victoria. The life of the sons, especially
the heir apparent, of our Queen, promises to keep that universal
love which they have already obtained.
Englishmen love their Queen and all her family, in which
love the author heartily joins.

THE KING.

(THE FIRST PLANTAGENET.)

———◆———

ACT I.

SCENE I.

The KING alone, walks to and fro hurriedly.

KING. Alone! now free from varied insolence
And fashioned flattery of crafty priests;
And yet my spirit jousts 'midst reveries,
Parries with shades and wan uncertainties,
Which waste this poor mortality.
But I will rend aside the trembling veil,
And summon to the footstool of my soul
My traitorous kin, and some too near my throne.
Come forth, my enemies!—Roger of York,
Bertrand de Born, Viscount de Hautefort,
Bold Strongbow, Pembroke, and wild Salisbury;
My ingrate sons, and my fanatic Queen;
That hardy fool, the restless heir of France;
Thou haughty saint, the Primate of my land,
The leader of this bold perfidious band.

[Pauses.

Perhaps sweet sleep may lull my weary brain.

[Here KING pauses, lies on couch, soon starts up.

The air seems panting with inanity,
Save sounds now buzzing round like merry bees

1

Returning from an unctuous festival,
Or some wild troop of gnats, at evening's tide,
Involved in orgies and in mystic dance,
With frantic chaunt, or dull weird monody.

[*Pauses.*

Perhaps the voices are to rouse e'en me,
And bear some messages from far-off worlds.
Ye mimic beings, whisper lowlily,
Say what shall sad to-morrow bear for me?
Shall I be spirit then, or be a king?
A king! that phantom thing! struggling awhile
To worst black Death, and hug a crown of
　　　　thorns!
A maniac's joy! Alas! I wish 't were o'er,
And I could sleep to wake no more.
But sleep deserts me now, hath joined my foes,
Or fears my soul is feigning weariness,
And that my dreams may murder sleep,
And tear it into dozing lassitude,
Or 'whelm it in some boiling cataract,
Or waft it up some craggy height;
Then urge it to the bottom of the sea,
To watch the sullen monsters roaming there.
Thus drive it mad 'midst strange discordancy,
Writhing with wild and hateful fantasies,
All incubate with turbid misery.
Ye spirits, provident in all. Oh! list,
And kindly yield these trembling lids some rest.
Yea, yea, until the great archangel shouts,
And the loud seraphim resounds the cry,
"Awake from mazy earthliness. Awake! awake!"

[*Pauses.*

O Sleep! thou lord of dark forgetfulness!
Unloose thy golden gates—a king now pleads—
(A warrior weary of blood-guiltiness)—

In soft petition as a gentle maid,
And promises no wantonness or sloth.
Bowed down, I seek a grave in thy domains,
And there in confidence forget my foes,
Whilst ceaseless storms of ill roll on their way.
The everlasting sleep must end my woes ;
Then revelations grand will be declared—
Eternal life unravelled as a scroll,
And immortality will wear its robes
Of righteousness. In that palatial home
I will forget the wrongs of earthliness,
And thus be conqueror in heaven and earth.
Transporting thought ! to tread upon this dust
And all the ruins of exulting Time,
And share the wonders of Omnipotence !

> [*After this soliloquy the* KING *lies on couch, and sleeps. The* ARCHBISHOP *enters unheard, stands looking on the* KING.

SCENE 2.

A BECKET. The tiger tired—hard hunted by
        the dogs,
Now driven to his lair—his sleep is deep,
And all the turbulence of time stands by :
His great resolves are waiting his command,
To manifest their fearless lord's behests.
Well, well—all well—a fitful dream—then death—
A sure release e'en to Ambition's child.
'T is well 't is so ordained by gracious Heaven.
If so, then why not now ? Ah, no ! not yet.
> [*Listening.*
Hark ! hark ! I hear some step—who's there with-
        out ?

No! no! 't was but the morning breeze hied by,
Or frighted doe, shivering with night's cold dew,
Embrangled in the arms of the stout oak,
Whilst rushing through the woods to welcome
  morn,
Encompasséd, like me, for present time.
Now Fear, thou myth, thou wanton, stand aside,
And take thy place with cowardice and sin.
'T was only Nature's lonely sigh! Conscience, be
  still!
Awhile relenting here, shining blade—not now.
'T is true 't would haste to heavenly rest; but, but—
          [Pauses.
I was thy friend—and thou dost call me friend;
But rocks and sands have riven our fair course.
Hadst thou been firm and fixed in thy resolves,
I should have ever loved proud majesty;
But pale expediency has led thee, king,
So looking on the surface of men's eyes—
And listen to the music of their tongues.
Until thyself hath meekly mocked thyself,
And left thee abject to their ends.
And now thy simulations are too late.
Thy strife for power, its shadow thou shalt have:
Its substance is in this pale palm intact.
       [Pauses, and looks on dagger.
This would suffice and reconcile us well.
But stay! another time—by other hands,
In tournament, or mazy dance, or broils,
Or e'en warm spice is sedative.
No, I'll not kill thee, king! Sleep soundly
  now,
And may wild antics in thy brain rebel
And ravage through the channels of thy life,
Until o'erwrought, madness set up a throne,

And jangles with ferocious gibes and whines,
Whilst midnight miseries confront thy soul.
Yet thou shalt have a wakeless sleep—more deep.
The Ides of March will soon come wheezing
        here ;
Meanwhile, thy sins will ravel up. Sleep on,
Besotted with thy dreamy banqueting,
Or rollicking in vacancy. Beware!
Oh, mystery! I see gay beams of smiles await
On that too living face, my enemy's,
And joyaunce rushes forth as ardent youth,
Or romping kid on Ida's lofty peak,
As though thy life were guiltless as a babe's.
But greedy fiends shall vault from worlds of fire,
Disporting round thy brow in ribbéd delves,
And stay thy prurient breath, thou heretic!
See! see! He frowns!—he menaces!—he wakes!
                [*The* KING *gradually awakes.*

  KING. What! kill by stealth! what! tilt for royal
    blood
E'en on my couch! Great Heaven! 'tis morn!
    I 'm free—
Free from the frowning spirits I have seen :
This feverish night has wearied me, o'erwhelmed.
E'en proud futurity disclosed strange secrecies :
The long-since dead filed slowly in my path,
The clanking bones of the first Conqueror
Stalked forth—he seemed to pass contemptuously,
Dumb, pale, with languid gait—proud ghost!
I thought I was in France, near blood's affrays,
Scuffling 'midst arms and reckless violence :
Vain Richard's heavy axe waved o'er my brow.
But in another dream fair forms appeared :
I saw the gates of heaven so gently oped,
And soon a group of fays descending thence,

Singing soft songs of their eternal life.
Ah, me! how sweet is peace e'en in a dream!

Enter OFFICER.

OFFICER. My liege, the hour appointed has arrived
And the battalions now are marching near.
KING. The lustrous sun now blushes for a king,
And chanticleer struts forth to sound my shame.
Awake, dull soul! renew thy toil of blood!

[Soldiers *appear. Drums heard.* KING *starts.*

Another time. Let drum and fifes now cease.

SCENE 3.

WALTER MAPES. The warrior Saul asked Music's
　　　noble voice.
KING (*excited*). But Saul's were wars with the
　　　Almighty One.
I have not tempered ears for dainty strains,
Nor simpering notes of soothing lullaby,
Which stay the motion of the angry will;
But I would list the raging breath of storms,
In concord with that drear and ruffled state
In which that priest would bait kind royalty.
Oh, for a muse of fiery elements!
To fright the caitiff and false hierarchies
Into that dark abyss they contemplate
As resting-place for me and all I love.
Stay, drum and fife, now mocking my resolves.

The QUEEN, DUCHESS DE BRETAGNE, *and* Courtiers *enter.*

KING. There comes the queen—the Duchess de
　　　Bretagne comes too:
QUEEN. Stirring by times, beloved majesty.

KING. These times are stirring, too, for majesty.
> [*Looking towards the* DUCHESS.

All hail to thy sweet voluntary here!
The duke is well—those eyes dispel all fear.

DUCHESS. 'T is well with priests, 't is ill with
royalty :
Take heed the springes of rebellion near
The prince! and priests are fashioning thy bier.
Look now!—see! see! thine enemies are there.
> [*Her eyes glisten with tears.*

KING. Oh, weep not here! lest those warm tears
of faith
Should melt repute, and leave me here suspect.

DUCHESS. Kind love 't is weeps for kinder
royalty,
And breeds deep anguish in my mourning soul.
I now will tell thee what my demon* warns :
" The brave oft meets what oft the brave oft scorns."
> [*Gives letter.*

Good king, read quick; there's travail for thy
strife,
Lest dark conspiracy shall seize thy life.

KING. Fear nought! Plantagenet defies the
world.

DUCHESS. My liege, in the grey morn I saw
the priest
Under the casement of her majesty
Counting his beads thus hurriedly—then stopped :
Such dreadful frowns stood on his angry brow,
Like crests of ocean's waves in turbulence ;
And once he started as though death had come,
And witches whispered some dire ministry,—
Walked on, stamped vehemently, looked around :

---

* See Note at end.

He seemed to balance to and fro some thought.
O king, I do conjure thee, king,—beware!
A woman's eye, untainted by this world,
Is 'luminated by the stars of heaven,
And they are fed by angels' hands.   Beware!
  KING. 'T is angry ill; yet from that silver voice
It seems not ill companioned in that light
Which on that brow enthroned entrances me.
Accept this ring for love's fidelity.
   DUCHESS. We now outstand good time.   Beware
     for aye!
Spices are well in wine—not well for thee;
They give strange rheums to noble majesty,
Which often lead to deathly casualty.
Farewell to sovereign ears—dull walls can see,
The queen's soft step moves on so stealthily.
   KING. Farewell!   Kind angel, fare thee well
    awhile!   [*Turning to* MAPES.
Now, wise and learned priest, cease praying here,
And sin elsewhere, as priests so well know how.
  MAPES (*leaving*). My liege's will commands me
    hence.
  KING.   Ah! ah!
The flood of holy thought must halt awhile,
E'en as the dead do rest in purgatory.

SCENE 4.

PETER OF BLOIS *comes in.* KING *holds up letter, much excited.*

  KING. I am deceived; the wolf has left his lair:
Now, soul, sail fast on this wild hurricane,
Laden with fire.   Stand back, Mortality,
And let this spirit bathe in crimson tides,
Where traitors' blood in many an alcove hides.

How little did the First Henry opine
What ills would come with legates sent from
    Rome!*
These bloody wars are bred by Rome's intrigues;
Its dastard craft o'erweaving all our state.
This burning blade may cut its way too late:
All ease and mirthful hours must now break up.
Awake! awake!—the Primate plays me false:
My crown is envied by the Vatican.
Awake, dull soul! and gird thine armour on;
Thy rest is o'er, the war is now begun.
But woe to all who dream that I can sleep
Whilst wolves and glistening snakes range o'er this
    land.
Now majesty stalks forth, defying fate.
    PETER OF BLOIS. Could noble majesty confide—
        once more?
Oh, stay! and explicate what haste might hide.
    KING. This sword shall explicate all treacheries
Now in the bowels of hypocrisy.
Stay!—ask the angry Mameluke to stay!
List to that wild reply o'er burning Araby
(Swift as the lion on his prey it comes;
Sure as the thunder follows lightning's torch):
"Stand back! I seek my country's enemy!"
Now every priest from every land shall learn—
Ay, learn, and teach to all, to understand
'T is death to disobey the king's command:
All shall obey the will of proud England.
    PETER OF B. Heaven's arm is ever on the side
        of kings.
    KING. The greatest power is in the hand of God,
And far afield from priestly truculence.

---

* Henry I. was the sovereign who first permitted legates from
Rome.

PETER OF B. But thou hast powers of state
　　await thy will.

KING. Nay, call them forms of power, which oft
　　prove vain—

Oft lie about as glittering garniture
For holidays and summer parasites.
Some power is weighed, and has a price in gold;
And some is used as wages for vile sins:
With priests 't is oft a venal prostitute—
Makes gibes, sells condiments and counterfeits,
Seduces with the serpent's tongue the poor,
Hiding its form 'midst absolution's clefts;
And thus supplant the law's resolve.

PETER OF B. Great king! thy power is infinite
　　on earth,

And powers unseen will regulate all else.

KING. Such platitudes are never worth their birth.
I know there is a Power bright and free—
Its being traces from eternity;
'T is seen in dignity and awful pomp,
When the Almighty, from His jasper throne,
All glorious moves. Mine ever cumbent lies
As vassal; yet 't is mine own—all mine—
'T is mine, by man and Heaven's appointment—
　　mine!

PETER OF B. 'T is thine, great king!—incarnate
　　robe!—all thine!

KING. This priest would steal it and deform the
　　world.

'T is mine, and this it shall be whilst I am—
'T is precious in my sight.

PETER OF B.　　　　　　My gracious liege
Will bear the fickle changes of this world:
'T is Heaven marks out those worthy of such
　　wrongs,

And leaves the worthless to fade slow and die—
Become pestiferous in sultry suns.
So mark, the rustling children of the wood—
Under whose shade the fairies dance at eve,
When gay Apollo sinks in western seas—.
E'en die, the sport of every gamesome wind.
Oh, let not royal hands in anger fold,
Or spread their power to gratify revenge!

KING. Oft have I heard thee say that every sin
May absolution gain; the sins of kings
Are noted nought; sins of the dazzled eye
Effaced; the tongue's foul eloquence made dumb;
And the polluted porches of the ear
Swept out, and, as a temple, purified.

PETER OF B. 'T is true, my liege; the dew of
        Heaven falls free,
Ah, yes! into the sacred hands of Rome,
Whence every earthly sin may be absolved.

KING. Yet there are sins unnatural and base,
Which make my kingdom rank and nauseate.
How many murders has De Lucey traced
To sundry priests? The civil arm shall reach
These holy murderers! Now ponder, priest!

PETER OF B. I would obey my king. I sorrow
        much.

KING. Thou know'st the length and breadth of
        England's lands
Are in surveillance to thy brethren.
·'T would seem that neither love, nor gold, nor fame
Can make my people free. 'T is strange, Sir Priest!
Oft would I firmly grasp this sullen foe;
But, as a spirit flies, he 'scapes my thrust.
He seems to lie in woman's eye as smiles;
In warriors' brows as harsh and haughty power;
In gold, from ingot's bar to tiny coin;

He hides and waits in glistening scaly form,
In dreams, in wars, in gallant tournament.

PETER OF B. My noble king sees shadows
    flickering.

KING. Ye priests but live with shadows simpering,
Floating in air—fearing to touch this earth.

PETER OF B. The Church oft mourns when royal
    sorrow sighs.

KING. A seeming mourning—oft-successful garb!
But penetrable by thy monarch's eye.
I 've seen my foe pass by me with disdain.
Sometimes he wears the sackcloth of the poor,
And oft the chaplet of the brave he wears;
In buzzing crowds of serfs and soldiery,
In fairs and hucksters' booths and mummers' troops,
This foe creeps in and grins upon my state.
My angel tells me in my fitful thoughts,
" These are the missions sent from holy Rome "—
Bear spice for some, narcotic draughts for some,
And storied absolutions perfumed oft;
For some, bright gems—ay, diadems for some;
For some—for me they bear a poignard, priest,
To help me on my way to purgat'ry.

[PETER OF BLOIS *leaves.*

SCENE 5.

The KING *and* WALTER MAPES *return to palace.*

KING. Well, happy Gollias, we would be gay;
But these rank priests, thy brethren, all toil
To make me sad, and puzzle my sick brain.

MAPES. Some virtues need much time to be ap-
    proved.
I do confess, some flowers are slow to bloom;
The storms of passion spoil their radiance.

KING. Walter, some day, far hence, in majesty
We may sit down with all the thousand tribes,
And judge these recreant priests! But now—
But now, just now, we must be chill and meek.

A C T I I.

SCENE I.

KING *and* SIR RICHARD DE LUCEY.

KING. Sir Richard, now at highest premium
Your mystic art appears. A king's reward
To rout—ay, instantly—from forth his web,
Bedabbled deep in varied treason's wiles,
A bloated monk, now loathsome to my sight!
What of our royal summons to this priest—
This great example of dark treason's ways?
    SIR RICHARD. It is reported he is sick and
        sad :
Some say that Hermitage delays his steps.
    KING. But who's without? List! 'T is the priest
        himself!
I know the gait and rumour of his step.

             [À BECKET *appears with* Retainers.

À BECKET. E'en now my liege's humble servant
        here,
Has dragged these weary limbs, now failing fast,
To be revived e'en in the presence air
Of royalty, so gracious, comely, just!
    KING. Sir Priest, 't is well! I wish the vulgar
        voice

Would tell some tale of honour of ye priests,
And that this sinning world, less reprobate,
Could see one heavenly ray or honest grace
In thine abundant comeliness.
    À BECKET. When virtue's lovers so fastidious
        grow,
The eye is querulous, the ear wide opes,
And fashions shadows into substances.
What need, my liege, to aid a vulgar broil
With me?—with me thy best, thine earliest friend?
This leads to woes immedicably wide—
Too wide for puny hands of kings to close;
Whilst vulgar eyes and ears waylay all state.
But know, I am the Primate of this land,
The only mission of great Heaven's high court!
Protector of the rights, all paramount,
Of the eternal world! Consider this!
    KING. Let prudence with thine eloquence keep
        pace!
Be frugal of thy words; for present time
Admits no idleness or wandering.
True grace is wanting, and a patriot's fear.
    À BECKET. Fear me! I can destroy thy soul,
        proud king,
And plunge this land in solemn interdict,
And close the gaping grave of heretics,
Defying thee and all thy fuming powers.
    SIR R. My lord, the king commands your pre-
        sence here
To-morrow's morn, John Marshall, knight, to meet.
    KING. Yes, yes! Thine eloquence may stead thee
        then.
    À BECKET. What revolutions are in state!
    KING.   In priests,
With innuendoes oft and trait'rous hearts!

Away! thou ingrate faithless priest! Go forth
And rule thy mythic world, and tyrannize
Amidst the herds of sleepy sensual knaves,
Whose lewd and murderous ways do plague my
    land!
Take heed, thine eminence is dangerous now:
The civil arm will execute its vow;
A cloud is in the heavens will strike thee low!
Thy lust for power is flaming on thy brow.
    À BECKET. I leave thee, recreant king—poor
        heretic!
Thy courage soon shall faint, I swear, I vow!
Thy troubles now will very quickly grow!

SCENE 2.

À BECKET, *disguised as a Knight, visits* PETER OF BLOIS.

À BECKET. A knight without, from holy Rome,
Demands thy fealty.
    PETER OF B. Thy mission, knight?
À BECKET. Peter of Blois, the Church requires
        thy faith.
    PETER OF B. The Church commands my faith,
my love, my life!
    À BECKET. 'T is well! Be true and firm, and
        steady too,
Nor blench at services Rome now commands,
To bear the vengeance of the holy Church.
Dost hear?
    PETER OF B. I hear; but all to me is mystery.
    À BECKET. Whilst I relate thy work (look not
        at me)
Which holy Rome demands forthwith by thee.
It must be soon—not slow—p'r'aps suddenly;
For scruples oft creep warily. Now list:

I bear great honour, gifts, and grants for thee,
For which some saints yearn anxiously.

PETER OF B. I am a poor and very humble priest,
Seeking but Heaven's great rest and earthly peace;
I pray for Heaven's Vicegerent twice a day,
And fifty paternosters have I said
That holy light may veil the Primate's path.

À BECKET. 'T is well. The Primate is great
      Heaven on earth.
Be sober. Mark! I list no canting now.
My mantle tells you I 'm a holy knight;
My. purpose is with death and silent tongues.
We want no pallid doubts what steel can do,
Or pleasant draughts inducted by the true.
Thou often art confessor, that I know :
The wafer is a boon of dying love
From sacred hands, it comes direct from heaven :
In that, thou know'st, some spice is often given.—
Don't stare at me as though I were the devil !
Nor breathe so hard, as though about to cavil :
Not me, the Church requires this good or evil.
'T is said the great Plantagenet is sick at heart—
(Perhaps gay Rosamond betrays his strength)
                            [*Aside.*
Some say he sinks, and you are complicate.

PETER OF B. I ? I ? He is my sovereign, and
      kind.

À BECKET. Which makes you stupid, obstinate,
      and blind.
Be kind, and humour all his mortal lust ;
But mark—the Church. requires thy fealty first.

PETER OF B. I 'm in bewilderment. I love the
      Church,
And every holy feature of its face.
O Mary ! angel of my life ! uphold !

Seraphs and saints, and all possessing souls,
Divert this holy knight from this affray!

À BECKET. Wake up, thou sulky monk!—thy
reverie
May cost thee much : 't is prurient artifice.
I 'll find thy betters—better for my end.

PETER OF B. Oh, hear my humble vow. I swear
to love——

À BECKET. Don't trifle with a soldier of the
cross.

PETER OF B. Oh! say what a poor monk can
do for Rome.

À BECKET. *(aside).* He relents! Why, mix nar-
cotics for a wakeful king,
And see he swallows portions well within,
That nothing dribbles from his wanton lips;
See that he swallows quick, and not in sips;
Sleeps deep and deeper still—and never wakes!

PETER OF B. *(pretending to misunderstand and to turn the
conversation).* I hear the king is well, so rumour says.

À BECKET. Rumour's a fool, and idiots love its
ways!
Come, monk, awake, and serve the Church, or die.
For seeking royal life thy life must pay.
I can be saint or vouch complicity :
The king will take my word and fealty,
And I can swear to thy hypocrisy.
Your body's mine,—the Pope may have thy soul.
List, monk, be Christian and philosopher.
Man toils in dust and shadowy scenes—in dreams.
And oft a deep dense sleep of nothingness.
Some are but blots on sweet creation's face.
The race of royalty is sad disgrace,
All swathed in clouds of lusts' anxieties :
Now help this "gallant king," far off, to heaven.

3

PETER OF B. I know all men must die; yet,
      awful thought!
That all must pace the vale of death—alone!
Then sin, unhappy sin, will have no cloak,
Or cowl, or knight's gay dress to hide awhile.
  À BECKET. Tush! simple fool, some even yearn
      to die.
Let his bold sprite rise there, for there 'tis wanting,
And with thy lips seal idle news withal,
And let the world's vile tongue wag on and on :
He's worth more sorrow than he now receives ;
Besides, he'll verify what oft he doubts.
There's nothing worthy in mortality ;
E'en life's a toy.   Now haste, and let him die !
Smothered in errors oft,—now brave, now weak,
Hasten the goal which all that's noble seek.
  PETER OF B. The ills I see now fill my heart
      with fear.
  À BECKET. He who is slave of fear is the wan
      fool
Who fails and follows shadows anywhere :
In many a rueful way he stumbles in ;
He feigns to be a saint when black in sin.
Once more take heed, thou painted hypocrite!
Thou dotard, listen now—confess I'm right.
Reply, if thou art able, instantly !
A curse is on thy couch : if thou shalt die,
Accursèd thy unprofitable store,
Though grasped within thy bony hands so twain !
Thy dream is nearly o'er, thou fool !   [*Aside.*
Another tack, and then he's Rome's sure tool.
Thou undone knave ! consider well thy fate !
  PETER OF B. Let spirits' aid, not man, or knight,
      or priest,
Make sorrow for the soul, unholy feat !

À Becket. Consider, priest, with thy rare intel-
    lect :
The wave is never weary of the winds,
But in bold playfulness leaps haughtily,
To join a freedom from the sullen calm,
And rides in state upon the hurricane ;
Exchanges fervent looks with the bright stars,
Companionizes with the lonely moon,
And whispers many a melody to night,
Whilst they descant on vain mortality ;
Thus doth the soul exult in every power,
Where, free from gloomy fashion's earthliness,
 Mind makes its own infinity
Complete, as in the twinkling of an eye.
    Peter of B. Oh, why discourse to me so learn-
        edly ?
    À Becket. To free a king from sad delirium
And slow decay of earth—humiliating—
With miserable chills—unconsciousness—
And all the hue and cry of gasping death !
To raise him to the eternal lights at once,
Where he may bask for never-ending years—
Visions on visions waiting on his soul—
Inducting to sublimity and peace.
    Peter of B. If I can serve the king I will.
    À Becket.   Tush ! tush !
Well ! well ! make haste to help a king to heaven—
A mortal king, with many mortal toils—
Distracted worm ! so pale, insensate, too,
As e'en the chilly marble of some god.
His presence in this world is not required,
His absence by the Church is much desired ;
His body yet remains, his spirit gone.
Come, priest, thou know'st the ins and outs of life ;
And matter hath so many qualities :

Part lives too long, and wants a friendly hand :
Here is thy warrant, opportunity, and all :
Thy chill effeminacy will serve no cause.
Take him to Mother Valley's pious hall,
And, if thou hast the courage of a fly,
Don't lose the golden opportunity.

    PETER OF B. Indeed I am an infirm instrument,
        I am.

    À BECKET. Then urge some drunken monk to
        some affray,
And charge he killed the king, and hie away ;
Or if in cups the king drinks greedily,
Then use thy wits and spices easily,
And charge it all to Val's iniquity.

    PETER OF B. I know no exercise in such sad
        broils.

    À BECKET. Be boisterous—ay, and e'en indig-
        nant, monk ;
Be sober in thyself ; if need be, drunk.
I leave thee now—a fortune in thy palm.
Whate'er thou dost, strike home : be steady, firm.
I 'm off till midnight ; then I 'll seek thee, monk,
To tell me if, in cups or else, he sunk.
But if thou fail'st, thou mimic murderer,
Thine hours are few, and I 'm no flatterer.

                    [*Leaves, saying,*
This monk is over-honest and a fool ;
I 'll find a substitute in Father Gull.

SCENE 3.

PETER OF BLOIS *alone.*

    PETER OF B. Oh, sad necessity ! I kill ? Never !
        never !
Oh, sad the will that wills my soul to sin,

And fall a victim as a regicide.
Can I forget this scene ?—perhaps a dream.
I 'll hasten to my sovereign this eve,
Then visit Mother Val's in deep disguise,
For some scenes there may ward off sad surprise.
Perhaps the holy knight may go himself,
To meet some substitute—some murderer.
I feel my spirit fail ; thought over thought
Now curdles in quaint mass my trembling blood.
That death is a necessity, I know :
To goad that awful minister of Heaven
Is not for knights, or priests, or any man.
I 'm not afraid of death—so oft a friend
In dreadful throes of wan mortality.
Death will and must bow this poor being down,
As dew the grass ; then comes another life,
Where pastures greèn and Rose of Sharon blooms ;
And then, the wondrous Majesty unseen,
Shall wipe away the varied tears of time.

À BECKET, *disguised, returns suddenly.*

À BECKET. Now, if thou art a man, be ready
    now.
Dost thou love woman, monk, with frail desires ?
I know a treasured nun not quite a saint,
With quaint deliciousness no eye hath seen—
A wondrous feast for long oft-waiting love.
She is the model of the beauteous Eve,
With fragrance of the timid jessamine,
That sweet perfection of a tender form,
And all the revelations tending there,
With queenly soul engraved o'er all her mien :
She is the mistress of the wanton king.
Now, wouldst thou give a truce to speciousness,
Ay, in the face of very loveliness

Exceeding all our wild conceit—ay, more—
I 'll lend thee armour stern and bright
To aid thy venture—ay, this very night.
Betray that nun—that's saying "if thou canst;"
But if thou fail'st, yet say that thou hast won,
And from her quietude export some test—
A handkerchief, or any under-vest;
Then on the wings of winds inform the king—
Make money, man, and misery of this thing.

    PETER OF B. *(aside).* This knight is cold blood
        guiltiness itself:
He would seduce the angels up on high.

    À BECKET. Thou frozen, pale, cold knave, be
        warned—take heed!
Or feel the ways of vengeance and their speed.

    PETER OF B. All seems confusion, giddiness, and
        dark.

    À BECKET. Thou fool! why take plain things
        too soon to heart?
What cunning musing now?—art faint or drunk?
Can unsubstantial death alarm a priest?
We all must yield our fashions unto mire
Ere we can hope to end this weariness,
And all the penitential throes of time.

    PETER OF B. My spirit fails, and thought o'er
        thought leaps forth;
Like burning waves they dash upon my soul.

    À BECKET. Thou crafty monk, I spend my time
        for nought.
What is there in a king—to Rome a foe?
Come, rouse thyself—from this faint dream awake.

    PETER OF B. Why talk as one who never loved
        a king
Of such proud parts and royal eminence,
So generous and confiding in his ways?

Alas! the dogs that fawned upon his state,
And licked the very feet of monarchy,
Wear traitorous hearts and dark ubiquities.
 À Becket. Away! away! some duties call me
   hence :
I 'll seek another aid with less pretence.

Scene 4.

King *and* Walter Mapes.

 Mapes. There is a scene this eve would tell
   strange tales :
'T would make the eyes of majesty stand out.
 King. But where, and when, and how could I
   survey
The merry monks who pray so heartily ?
They know my bearing well.
 Mapes.   Leave that to me.
The merriment this night is opportune.
Where foreign monks carouse and spend their gold,
I 'll lead my liege right in the midst of all,—
Yes, at the house I know : 't is old Saint John's.
I 'll show at once the passions in full play,
At summit all, with all their hectic glow,
And burning glance, which ever radiate
The brow of sin which wars against the soul.
 King. 'T is well : I 'll join this happy scene this
   night,
And view these sage Italian monks in cups.
What order shall I be—Cistercian ?
 Mapes. Capuchin will be best becoming thee :
I 'll make thee priest. I 'll come, my liege, at ten,
Unless some murderer shall step between.

SCENE 5.

Monks *and* Cavaliers *carousing in a Tavern.*

ANSELM DE BURGOS (*throwing himself back in his chair*).
I hear some news—À Becket fights the king!
Tell me what all this means—say, Godrich, say.
 GODRICH (*rather drunk*). The king is mad, and kicks
  against the pricks,
As some wild colt he wrestles with his lord.
 ANSELM DE B. He's sick with love, and passion
  rules his life.

A Cavalier *near.* FATHER GODRICH, *who is drunk, takes up
his hands.*

SONG BY ALL VOICES.

(*Sings.*) A bumper of good liquor
  Will end a contest quicker
  Than justice, judge, or vicar:
   So fill a cheerful glass,
   And drink to the fair lass.
  But if more deep the quarrel,
  Then quickly drain the barrel,
  That's for the stupid fellow
  That's crabbed when he is mellow.
   Then let the glass pass,
   And drink to the lass, &c.

CAVALIER. Ye learned friars, just list to me
  awhile;
This is the holy priest who seldom prays,
Yet often fasts until his hunger comes,
And never drinks except the wine be good.
He is the Pope's vicegerent—well employed.

    [*The* Monk *falls on the floor, tipsy.*

He's sleepy now; but that's the fault of wine!
Some day he'll be archbishop, so they say,
And find us merry souls another way
To heaven; and all I say I wish he may.

   [*Turns his empty glass on the face of the fallen* Priest.

Here's holy water, which I pour on thee,
And make St. Osith's priest thus consecrate.
All who can stand, now join your hands with me,
And let us dance and sing right merrily !   [*Sings.*

> Here's Hermitage and Burgundy so bright,
> Which makes old joys return, and woe so light.
> That like a feather it goes dancing by,
> To seek a bed in some fair maiden's eye,
> And gives to loveliness a pensive dye,
> And heaving cadence to soft minstrelsy !

Enter KING *and* WALTER MAPES *as foreign Monks.*

MAPES. All happy souls who quaff old Vally's
    wine !
KING. 'T is wine which washes sin into the veins,
And drives men on to Pluto's gloomy shade.
See ! see ! these priests seem sliding in apace.
MAPES. Ah, yes ; they drink of Sodom's feverish
    wines,
And waste their strength to drink Gomorrah's gall,
And thus fall into Hades after all.

VALLY, *the Hostess, appears.*

VALLY. Good holy fathers, ye are welcome here.
What generous wines shall tempt your sacred lips ?
'T is heaven-born liquor—take my word for that.
MAPES. Good Mother Val, your guests are rather
    gay :
They sing so loud I cannot hear them pray.
VAL. The night is early yet ; we soon shall have
The fairest dames who live in palaces ;
A noble holy knight from Palestine,
With cavaliers and many pious souls ;
And I expect the Pope this very night,
And many fair less rigid to the sight.
Some come to speed a royal soul to heaven—
The doating lover of Fair Rosamond.

4

She's very handsome, so I've heard men say;
Her eyes make darkness bright as any day.
Such form! such fashion!—I have seen this maid:
Fair as the moon, and knows as many things.
She's never condescended to come here—
Perhaps 't is innocence.

KING.   Perhaps 't is fear.

ACT III.

SCENE I.

ROSAMOND, *in bower, sings.*

Whilst the dull breeze is whispering lowlily,
And waits in Night's cold arms alone, like me,
Just where the moody owls in woods hard by
Wake echo from sweet mystic reverie,
I'll offer prayer for my dear prince away.

[Listens.

Hark! hark! I hear some step. 'T is phantasy,
Or the dry leaves in their wild roundelay,
Or timid sprite from dreadful scenes walks by.—
List! list!

ATTENDANT. That whining priest, who once con-
    fessed thy soul,
I do declare! Beware! beware! 'T is he!

ROSAMOND. Who? who? Say, man, who art
    thou? and from whom?

PR. Dear lady fair, the silver stars come forth,
Illume the devious path, when trembling hope
Bears heavenly news to sweet mortality.

Ros. But who art thou, intruding covertly?

PR. I come to join thy prayers—the evening
    prayers;

And will attend thee to confessional.

ROSAMOND *and* PRIEST *in Confessional.*

PR. Fair lady fair, say whence those pensive
    sighs,
Which add such beauty to those lustrous eyes ?
Perhaps remorse of some false step gone by
Makes beauty sigh ?
    Ros.   'T is sorrow makes me sigh.
    PR. Sweet beauty's sigh is sacred minstrelsy.
Why shouldst thou sigh so near the feast of love ?
Now, sweetest dreams should play in ecstacies ;
Now, love should spend its gallant holiday,
And spread its rare possessions free,
Regardless of the rapids of wild time.
    Ros. *(aside).* (Until that hour my precious prince
      returns).
Woe's heavy waves roll o'er my weary heart ;
In rightful majesty they take their course :
As tide of burning streams they dash o'er all,
And seem to tell of grief so drearily.
Until my prince returns—all mystery !
    PR. How strange that he should leave so sud-
      denly !
Hark ! hark ! the nightingale now tells her tale.
    Ros. Alas ! sweet bird, thy tender notes I hear :
Is it for love, or for some dreary woe,
Thy gentle notes now plead so very low ?
Oh, plead that England's noble king may live !
    PR. The brightest flowers are killed by earth's
      cold winds ;
And such are best in heaven.   For this oft pray.
    Ros. Wise priest ! I pray to Heaven incessantly.
    PR. Pray that the Primate's foes may fall !—say,
      Ay,—

Like autumn's faded flowers no more may rise.

[ROSAMOND *seems more amazed.*

Just list, fair nun, awhile, prepare thine ear :
Now be attent. Wise love grasps present time,
And breathes its perfumed life to audient ears,
Full sanctified e'en by our holy Church.
I come to soothe thy woes—no common guest ;
I come to shrive thy soul of every sin,
And seek the full confession of thy love ;
I come to bear full witness, if thou wilt :
Thou art with pious ornament replete—
To thee I bow : to love's eternal self !

[ROSAMOND *looks aside contemptuously.*

PR. (*aside*). I need the trappings and august
 display
Of chivalry and martial attitude ;
But loss in love shall buy me full revenge.

[ROSAMOND *looks round to* PRIEST *alarmed.*

'T is pious passion elevates my soul !
Say, shall its lustre shine in clouds and die,
Whilst Time's rough foot impairs its beauteous-
 ness,
And made to quiver like a midnight lamp,
Or live for ever bright in thee, sweet saint ?

[PRIEST *appears retiring.*

ROS. (*aside*). O love, thou wilderness of woe !
This priest assumes thy faint beatitudes ;
He would betray a sad and lonely one
Into some darkness now to me unknown.

[PRIEST *turns back.*

Sir Priest, disport not in this nether world :
Thy vows have made thee servant of high Heaven.
I do implore thy absence instantly !

PR. I do implore thee now. My love for thee

Is high as heaven—vast as eternity;
It lives, and ne'er, ay, ne'er can change or die.

[PRIEST *approaches* ROSAMOND.

Ros. I do adjure thee, priest, whate'er thou art,
Hast thou no reverence for mighty Heaven?
And dar'st thou hide thy vile intendments thus
In folds and palid comeliness?   Stand back!
What! in the sacramental garb thus act?
Stand back!   What evil spirit has seduced thee
       thus?
Those flickering lights are soon put out by this.

[*Points to her breast, shows dagger.*

'T is now I feel a sphere encircles us,
And that thine abject life is in my palm.
I will not let thee add besetting sins
Unto the catalogue of that gross heap
Which fester on thine ignominious heart.

    PR. Dear lady, do not sigh and groan with
       threats,
As though sweet love was in its mourning clothes,
Nor measure admiration's ecstacies
As high offence or dark designs on thee.
That I do love thee shall appear anon,
When I recount the virtues of our king,
Who reigns on thrones of loveliness,
Fair as the fairest flowers which deck the earth.
And one there is, arrayed in beauty's sheen,
With love that wins the heart it would upbraid:
He often loves, as rumour dares to say,
Some else—I 've heard soft names oft given;
The Stafford maiden's heart is somewhat riven.
Yes, passing life contains its varied gifts.
Fair Rose, 't is love's chief joy to live in loyalty—
    Ros. Such love and loyalty are virtue's fruits.
    PR. I often watch the beauteous stars above,

The pallid moon, the ever-restless sea,
The morning's earliest hour, its dainty dew—
All steal the sweetest of all worship—love,
And dress the panting heart in fervency.
    Ros. Such love and loyalty I well approve
Which wear the countenance of mighty Heaven.
    Pr. Oh, hear me, lady fair, I do implore!
                           [*Approaching her.*
    Ros. Priest! monk! stand back! Thou hideous
        monk, avaunt!
If thou hast prayers and homilies to say,
Be warned betimes, ere time has run away:
Thou art a traitor to thy king and God.
    Pr. The king is sad, in many dangers lives;
If dead, enthralled in war's uncertainties;
And dead men's love will barely suit good taste.
    Ros. (*excited*). But dost thou say he lives in heaven?
        or earth?
    Pr. If living, he must meet a direful doom.
Rebellion to the Pope kills many a king;
Has cost a thousand worlds of suffering:
Between the fires I see no way for him.
Strange beauties make some lovers wavering.
    Ros. (*alarmed*). Good priest, forget my past
        timidity;
But say—oh, say! what dost thou think or know?
(The king is true in all love's fealties,   [*Aside.*
And yet he seems oft laden with deep sighs—
Some strange surmises into body grow).
Oh, if my lord is ta'en to heaven—oh, say!
I will confess my heavy sins and die.
    Pr. Of this anon: this life is but a spark;
To-day it brightly shines, to-morrow, dark.
But now awake, and with all pleasantry
We'll pass the precious hour—both happily.

I 'll keep the secret safe from jealous eyes :
The Church has ways to lull all secrecies.

    Ros. My lord, great king, as ghost or bodily,
                     [*Shouts in excitement.*

Appear! avert this evil from thy love!
This vampire dares to violate thine own!

    Pr. Oh, come—now yield; live in my arms,
        sweet fair!

For thee I 'll yield eternal life—dost hear?
Oh, doubt not me! such passing sins ne'er fear;
I hold authority to stop the tear
Which timid conscience oft will seem to bear.
I am the Pope's familiar—don't fear: see this!
        [*Shows* Pope's *absolution for this and other sins.*

    Ros. (*aside*). Kind Heaven, forbid me falling here
        —alone.   [*Turns round, and vehemently stamps.*

Thou wily priest! thou shalt unfold my woe
In words distinct—ay, one by one. Now say—
Say what is in thine evil mind—oh, say!
For silence may thy mortal life betray.
Make haste, then, monk—eschew thy vile intents
(Come heaven, come earth, lend me thy mighti-
        ness!)
If thou hast love for gold or glistening stones,
Or rubies' brilliancy—oh, say the cost—
The price, however high; thy reticence,
Break that I will, or thou or I must die;
For time grows short—watch woman's trembling
        eye.   [*Shouts.*
Hear Madness cry; declare, thou hypocrite—
Reveal the secret thou wouldst meanly sell:
You trifle at the very gate of hell.
For crime so vast, and wanton villany,
Thy blood—thy putrid, rampant blood—shall
        cease:

'T is my turn now to have my great revenge.
If thou hast prayers to say, say instantly;
This anguish bears me in its stormy back,—
Make haste, thou caitiff—haste, or humbly die.

  PR. And if I tell thee all I know—what then?
Wilt thou abjure thy heresy in love?

  Ros. Beware! beware! I will not bear delay;
I 'll dash into thine eyes this liquid flame,
And stop those inlets to thy lustful brain.
See here, this smoking fire—my second aid;
Thou priest, beware! the cloud is o'er thy brow
(The opening light of heaven confirms my vow)
Which holds a thunderbolt to bear thee low.

       [*Pauses—walks with maniac step.*

Silence!   Sweet echo brings my prince — list!
  list!
Rejoice, my soul! I hear the tramping steed
Which bears my love to lonely love's great need.
Escape as for thy life—the king! the king!—
My precious ever-during love,—he comes!—

         [*Listens.*

I am deceived: it was the evening's breeze.

   [*The* PRIEST, *alarmed, tries to escape; but hides*
    in bushes near, and for hours.

  Ros. (*alone*). In what a mesh this timid spirit lies!
These feigning hypocrites! these whining priests,
They burrow far within, and soil the soul.
(That holy beauteous gift, companion fond!
That dove which mourns when cloudy sin appears.
As some hoarse hawk springs on his hapless prey,)
Wringing from thence its first, its holy love;
And then corruption desolates the whole.
O Mary! Holy Mother! shield thy child!
Ye myriad fires which walk the vaulted heavens,
Attend the thousand saints who sleep in peace,

"I am deceived: it was the evening's breeze."

p. 32

And rest insensate now to mortal woe,
Their labours o'er ; faithful have been their lives.
I come not to disturb ye, burning fays,
Nor ask the secrets of yon vaulted skies,
Which bound the spacious empire where ye roam :
I come to tell the winds and oozy tides,
Upon the frontiers of all hope I stand.
Ye starry lights, now be my witnesses :
I come to tell my woes, ye ministers of light ;
To you I would unfold my grief.
I seek a place of rest or some cold grave,
Which some wild waves might rock through
           endless time,
And gentle Vesperus might moan with me,—
A sea-girt grave, close by some rocky spot,
Where I might watch the secrets of the deep,
The gamesome stars and meteorous lights of
           heaven,
And wait until the wand'ring moon is up,
Walk forth and ponder by the sad sea-shore,
Then start e'en to my icy bed of death,
In reverie awful, no more to wake.

SCENE 2.

Enter KING *and* QUEEN.

KING. Good queen, thy earnest piety puts shade
On all the seemings of religious life.
  QUEEN. A holy life puts shame on piety ;
It is the refuge of mortality,
  KING. O thou hast heavenly love attending thee,
      good queen !
  QUEEN.   Love on earth, where pure,
Is heavenly love ; where forced, it is not love.

                  5

KING. The spirits pure revolve in perfect love;
But what is earthly love? This question oft
I poise and balance at my lance's end.
My chaplain says it herds amongst the sins.

QUEEN. Ah! be the owner of that holy joy
Which throbbing passion ever vainly seeks.
By loving, all may learn the answer true;
As the bold diver knows the white pearl's bed,
Whilst they who buy and sell this precious thing,
Know nothing of her deep and beauteous cell.
Love will exalt, although dependence comes
And forms its nature and its dignity;
As ivy o'er the castle turret high
Clings to the rugged wall; and whilst it yields,
It borrows strength from might and majesty,
And with its emerald cloak, in sombre guise,
It decks the noble pile of mother earth,
Diverts the sultry sun; and every storm
And hurricane but strengthens that embrace,
Which shall for ever last.

KING.   For ever? Ah!

QUEEN. Sire, yes; and when these stars and
            changeful moon
Have sunk within those far unknown degrees,
Still shall remain the sweet embrace of love,
Which shall for ever be.

KING.   For ever? Ah!
For ever is so very long, good queen!

QUEEN. As ever any earthly thing shall be.
But that tall castle height must fall;
The mountain where the golden sun has hid;
Those rocks, where lonely eagles, sullen, rest;
The peaceful valley, where the kine oft lowed;
The boundaries of the raging billow's crest;
The Pleiades and wild Arcturus, too,

"*O Love! thou inexpressible mystery.*"

Must render up their native majesty,
When the shrill trumpet of the angel sounds,
Which calls the wand'ring tribes of man to heaven.
But love's exhaustless song, all melody,
Shall lead the choirs of heaven's great palaces,
And in the presence of Almighty Love,
Shall sound its sweeter notes to angels there.
It is not long—it is no part of time.
 KING. Wise queen, thou shalt instruct me more
   at length ;
For I do love grave learning's depths and heights,
And schoolmen's difficult and knotty points.
I love romantic thought and heavenly recipes.
 QUEEN. No, no. I speak no more to thee ; 't is
   vain :
I leave thee with thy monitor within.
Stand well with that great company.—Farewell !

SCENE 3.

The KING *walking towards* ROSAMOND's *Bower.*

KING. O Love ! thou inexpressible mystery—
Oh, say, kind Heaven, and ye mystic things,
Why was I born with impulses so rare ?
Why born a king 'midst dark conspiracies ?
Why not some happy serf, with appetites
For ordinary boons and rosy healthfulness,
That neither love's entanglements, though sweet,
Nor pleasing hopes deferred, or pride dismayed,
Could tantalize in this strange pilgrimage ?
     [KING *pauses—hears a voice :*

 Near a tall distant tower,
  Where vesper bells were ringing,
 A fair maid watched in a lonely bower,
  Faintly and slowly singing.

I heard her song, sweet maiden fair,
As she passed her hand through her long fair hair :
   This trembling hand oft held by one
For whom my heartfelt prayer shall be ;
   But must I wait so long alone—
Say, angels, when will he return ?
A bounding step hastes near that bower,
Whilst quivering lips are singing lower.
She sighed no more—sweet, happy fair !
For the love who loved her with love was there !

SCENE 4.

KING *appears before* ROSAMOND, *whereupon she says :*

Ros. Awake, my soul ! awake ! Now contem-
      plate
The joys the presence of thy lord creates,
Which have no life in his long tarryings.—
But why, sweet love, so sorrowful ?
    KING (*sighs*). Ah ! ah !
    Ros. Perhaps some long vicissitudes have torn
That breast I loved to lean upon so oft.
    KING. Dear one, we would not mingle in this
      hour
The strifes and turmoils of this naughty world.
    Ros. Then stay that deep philosophy, which
      weighs
With secret power upon thy gentle breast.
I fear it often heaves when far away :
Thou dost not tell me, love, what makes thee sigh.
Is it the heaving of a storm gone by
That gives those glittering orbs that pensive dye ?
    KING. Well, yes. This heart has deeply sighed
      and heaved
Wildly, as some sore vexed and angry sea
Madly throws up its ancient firm foundation
In many countless dusky atoms, thickly,

Which hid the glorious golden sands below,
That sparkled in the sun of calmer days.

    Ros. (*in tears*). 'T is thus : thy brow has gloomy
       . spectres dark,
Which execute sad havoc on the heart.
Well, well! this misspent life is wearing fast.

    King. Life is a speck—a visionary spot ;
Or like a fragment or a splintered spar
Lent for awhile to sinking mariners.
Some buffet long—ne'er gain the distant shore ;
Some drift along the turbid tide alone ;
Some bound upon the beach triumphantly.

    Ros. My dearest one, I love to hear thee talk :
It elevates my soul to rapturous heights ;
But then come dull and stormy thoughts and fears.
Well, be it so! Bright life is fading now,
And soon comes peaceful death to hide e'en all ;
And then the resurrection comes, when Heav'n
Will give me back that pearl which, being lost——

    King. What pearl ? what pearl ? What means
       my Rosamond ?
What pearl is lost ? and where ? and when, and
       how ?
Through every land, o'er every sea I 'll roam,
Until I find the pearl my love has lost.

    Ros. It was a pearl of drifted snow, given me
By One who rules the heavens, the earth, the sea,
And before whom all kings must humbly stand.

    King. Some heavy woe disturbs my Rosamond.

    Ros. Oh ! 't is a woe no mortal hand can heal—
Not e'en my precious one's own hand :
It has eternal influence to wound,
Until one stream of anguish fills my soul.

    King. Sweet Rosamond, see! heaven's pale
       queen is up

To take her lonely course.   The sparkling stars
Will soon assemble round : be cheerful now.
    Ros. Ah ! ah ! 't is thus with man.   Woman to
        him
Is but a toy.
    King.   Thy pallid cheek alarms——
    Ros. The hour has come : I now will yield up
        all.
Monarch of heaven, I now will yield to thee !
These mortal eyes, which loved to glisten bright,
Feasting on all these kindred things, in midst
Of which I fell—fell !—are now immortal,
And ne'er shall glow again with finite joys.
Listen ! ye radiant beings bright—listen !—
Listen ! With you I 'll spend eternity :
To you I 'll chant sad melody—too sad
For mortal ears.   Alas ! sad minstrelsy !
    King. Dear Rosamond, revive—consider, love.
    Ros. I wait the blast which calls the wand'rer
        home :
I speak amid the ruins of my heart.
See ! watch the flames ! they burn as high as heaven,
And sorrow is my fated prophetess.
    King. Come, charm this human sorrow off, dear
        love :
How often we have met, and often may.
    Ros. We may !   Oh, faithless, fragile, hopeless
        hope !
I dash thee and thy opiate censer down
To that poor being who, well intending me,
Did win me from my heavenly path so far
To sink for ever-—alas, for ever !—love.
    King *(aside)*. Oh, now I feel the scorching fires
        of hell !
    Ros. Thus the green leaves of youthful life to die,

Entangled 'midst this pride and wild desire,
With them to putrify.

KING.   Oh, say not so!
Why wilt thou hug this sorrow, Rosamond?

Ros. It is my spirit and my angel now;
We live together in sweet confidence:
Disturb it not, my love, my ever-loving love!
Not one, but many thoughts, distract me oft.
E'en now let pale and greedy Sorrow hear;
Thou gentle spirit, hear e'en me.   Alas!
Listen!   Thou shalt have all these ashes—
To thee I yield these charms, though now so spoil'd,
Which made this mortal being loved and lost.
Ye aiding spirits—missions of kind Heaven—
Unloose this trembling, anxious thing—
This sister spirit take: it longs to fly;
For whilst it writhes, it longs to be released.
Oh, tender be! as your Creator, kind.
Farewell, dear king!   Until we meet in heaven,
Ten thousand years may roll in purgat'ry
Ere that bright hour shall be.   Dear king, farewell!

                    [ROSAMOND *reclines on couch.*

Left in this wilderness so oft alone—
A toy, or less, to be but gazed upon,
Now all the charms of life have fallen,
And nature's self is tattered and forlorn.
Farewell, good king! farewell to all—to all!

SCENE 5.

Enter ELEONORA, *the* QUEEN.

QUEEN. The king!   What! here?—is it the
         king himself?

KING. Madam, how came you here?   Answer
         me, dame.

Much difficulty to trace a path
So devious——

    QUEEN. (*showing a skein*). So devious!—yes, very
      so.
But see this faithful skein!—see here, wise king!
True lover's haste, forgetting bolts and bars,
Had left the drawbridge flagging to and fro.*
This pretty guide was honest, too, my lord!
With safety it hath led my timid steps
To one whom England boasts her king; to one
Who once did make this wild impassioned heart
Beat high and proud.—But I no more complain;
I see enough to excite my sorrow.
    KING.   Hold!
Madam, all this I can explain anon.
I do command thee hence; for, present time
Allows not explications various.—
Leave me, I say!
    QUEEN.   Nay, why so earnest, Sire?
Just now I saw commissioners from Rome,
And business brought me to sequestered parts—
I wished to see a king a-chambering.
                        [*Affecting to leave.*
I leave, I grant thy suppliant claim—I go.
Thou once my humble adoration held;
But the sweet glances of a dying nun,
Which well entreat such fitting company,
Have made thee truant, negligent, unkind;
But since thou lov'st, love still, I pray thee love.
I do e'en yet admire thy fortitude:
Thy majesty hath much endured, I fear?
Thy treasure there has cost thee watchings long,

---

    * The bower could only be ascended by a moveable draw-
bridge, which Henry II. had caused to be built.

Waitings, and kind sustainings, and the like.

KING. I look to see thee gone.

QUEEN.   Oh, do not look
This barren way ; for see, that lily pale
Threatens to sink again, and e'en will die
Without thine arm.

KING. Madam, I mark thy poisoned raillery.
Thy malice wears a proud crest, eminent
Above thy other passions numerous.
This lady is as favoured as a queen,   .
As honoured, as well-bred, as learned too ;
And wants no drop of gentle blood.

QUEEN.   *Sans doute !*
The lady you 've described with graphic touch—
For which her thanks abundantly are due—
Wants nought ; her wants are richly all supplied !
Her pearl-white hands oft well employed
To cool the fevered brow of gallant kings.

KING. Madam, I may do that which I would
      ·   not.

QUEEN. Is it, then, courteous to leave a nun,
A meek and fainting maid, to sink so low,
Without the delicate aids which her own sex,
Methinks, are meetest to afford ?   Well, well !
I will not blame—I rather pity thee,
A monarch great, encompassed as thou art.
And yet, O blissful state ! how fine the tie
That binds in secret bonds congenial souls !—
But see, my lord, that lady falls again.
Now she essays to speak.   Perhaps she seeks
The unction of the Church ?

                 [ROSAMOND *opening her eyes, unaware*
                      of QUEEN'S *presence.*

Ros.   Ah, that cold hand !
Remove its heavy palm : it drives me down'

                                     6

With more than lightning speed! Yct, yet I have
The fond assurance here that angels' love
Will bear me from this low abandonment
To those sublime and pure ethereal realms
That are too rarefied to bear the weight
Of sin, or pain, or penitential woe:
There all is lost in love, so pure, so great!
Hark! Heard you not that glorious voice? so
          sweet,
The seraphim? They call for Rosamond—
The guilty, sad, and wandering Rosamond:
"Return! return!" Hark! hark! Angels, I
          come,
To live with thee above, and grafted there
On stem no earthly power can dare to break.

> [*Wild and wandering, sees the* QUEEN.

Ha! ha! See there! Who's that? What do I
          see?
Is that dark gulf for Rosamond? Here! here!
Take me, some fury, now! Must I go there?
What! go to hell to find a refuge there
From the hot fire that burns within this heart,
And rase for ever from my maddened eyes
That sin I see as deed of yesterday,
When, deaf to all but passion's suasive voice,
I left the peaceful roof that sheltered me
In buoyant childhood's days of innocence?
Ah, ah! this weight of woe succumbs me quite.
Where can I lean? ye spirits say—oh, where?
The Church did promise to withhold this draught,
This bitter draught! Oh, faithless, faithless Church!
It vowed to blot all sins from memory.

> [*Seizes* HENRY *wildly.*

Is this, then, Death? Is this long-envied Death?

If so, I love thee, Death! I love thee, Death!
That e'en not Henry shall unknit this clasp,
Or tear thee, Death, from Rosamond!—But soft!

[*Passionately pushing* HENRY *aside.*

Hush! ye rude boisterous winds, and lightly blow;
And in soft dying cadence waft your wings
To your far-distant homes, where southern skies
Shed brighter beams upon the smiling earth—
Go! go where cascades clear and crystal streams
Did erst suppress their murmur sweet, to list
The sweeter sounds with which the Mantuan reed
All vocal made the sunny vine-clad hills
And orange bowers, so loved by Dryad nymphs.

[*Pauses.*

And now the shadowy vale is nearly passed,
And the bright confines of eternity
Before me shine. See, yonder now descends
The fairest, meekest of the spiritual world—
The herald Mercy, smiling through her tears.
Yes, yes! she's pointing to the spotless robe;
And all my accusers stand abashed and dumb:
The wicked priest who prompted me to sin,
Now bound in fetters in that dreary world
Where angry serpents, never ceasing, hiss.
See! see!—the angels beckon me—I come!
Now plume my wings to fly.—Where am I now?
In heaven, or earth, or purgatory's clime?
Now let this secret mystery be mine:
Shall I be welcome, or for ever cursed?

[ROSAMOND *reclines.*

KING This scene has wearied thee. Now rest
        awhile,
Sweet Rosamond! thou hast forgiving love,
And many smiles from spirits high in heaven,

Whilst every wave of time (some ruffled now)
Wafts thy kind heart to sweet societies,
Where fears of this cold world are hushed for aye.
And when the lingering sighs of life is still,
Thou wilt partake the sacrament of love.
To me each moment brings some torture fresh,
Which courses through my blood as denizen,
Bearing the anguish of that dreary state
To which I seem now driving on apace.

[ROSAMOND *sleeps.*

May angels guard thee, love! Farewell, farewell!
All hail! Great Master of all wand'ring earth!
Under Thy pall, Thy mystic hallowed vault,
The spirit there may fly 'midst curling clouds,
And scale the skies in its prerogative;
Or enter realms of fire, or beard the moon,
And list to sulphurous roarings underneath,
Above, and all around the murky world!
Then rest in Purgatory's arms, listening
To waves which ever beat on Lethe's shore.

ACT IV.

SCENE I.

QUEEN *alone, walking in Ditchley Wood.*

QUEEN. Long have I mused (as on a couch intent
Fair Dido let the proud Æneas leave
Her arms expanded for his noble love),
And thus this ambling doe escapes my toils.
I now throw back the curtain of delay;
But how?—but how? No room is left for doubt:

That must be quickly done which must be done.
Dull resolution lies on the back of time ;
As on a speck of land, 'mid boisterous seas,
Some shipwrecked treasure long neglected lies,
Whilst many suns and moons alternately
Glance by, and many a billowy tide bounds on,
Until some angry storm sweeps all away.
Thus change on change goes on, and chance is lost :
'T is now the king being absent for awhile ;
'T is now I may enfold this downy lamb
Within my longing arms, and then—ay, then !—·
I well may feast in all the rest of time,
When that blood chills which in its current dares
To gleam like rubies sparkling on the cheek,
As Hebe's fresh, of Rosamond the Fair !
Up, up, my daring soul !—up, up, I say !
Let fiends attend and gossip as we go—
Contend—dissent—agree—

FURIES *appear.*

Too-wit, too-wit !

The day is gone ; whilst Evening beckons Night
To array the concave heaven in funeral suit,
That Melancholy from her cell may step,
To indulge her dreamy thoughts and musings deep.
But night is bright, and day is dark, to Guilt,
Whose lidless eye owns not the boon of sleep.
Ye furies, blench not at the task prescribed,
But some wild song of hideous import chant.
But sing some dreary glee to please black Death.

FIRST FURY.

I sit by the forest pine,
    And dream of death and blood :
The realms of the future are mine,
    I float in its boiling flood.

SECOND FURY.

The speckled moon rides high,
  The gloomy fir rocks in her bed ;
And every angry wind that's nigh
  Is by a fiery demon led.

THIRD FURY.

I have poised in the trembling air,
  I have slept in the coral bed,
Where every glistening spar
  Shines on the putrid dead.

FOURTH FURY.

The sighing breeze with perfumed wing,
  That wantons o'er the plain,
Shall fan a victim's death-pale cheek,
  And Henry's reign be vain.

FIFTH FURY.

I sleep near the cataract's thunder,
  Within the lion's lair ;
Where the rocks are riven asunder,
  And forkéd lightnings tear.

SIXTH FURY.

As sure as morn shall gild the sky,
  Or rippling stream declare its course,
De Clifford's peerless child shall die,
  And die by vengeful woman's force.

QUEEN. Oh that the murky lamp of wandering
    fiends
Would gleam conductive on my devious way !
Oh ! how I long for proofs most palpable
Of Death's irrevocable work ! Yes, yes !
Let every sensual organ yield its share :
The fixed, the glassy, visionless eye ; the mouth
Half open, and the nostril gaunt, from whence
No breath of pride or grateful sweetness comes :
The bosom silent, marble cold, and still.
But I must haste, lest better angels come

With Mercy's palm, and stop this work of blood.
Come, tardy Death! here is my bright ally!

[Looks at dagger.

Or if my purpose turns, accounting well,
Here are more tender viands sparkling high.

[Holds up phial.

What holds me thus, and keeps me from my end?
Now, soul, be steadfast here. Long hast thou worn
An earthly crown : bright is that precious earth ;
But yonder lies a kingdom brighter far
Than Paradise. A waxen wall alone
'T wixt thee and thy long-sought possession stands.
But hark! It is the nightingale I seek.

The KING *approaches Bower.* ROSAMOND'S *voice is heard
singing.*

That morning's beam is gone
    Which shone at break of day,
And I am still alone—
    No ray for me!

Oh, do not change that face,
    Thou lonely murmuring stream !
Oh, do not lose that grace,
    O'er which I loved to lean.

I wish I had a grave
    Close by some rocky shore,
In madness there to rave,
    Nor think of Henry more.

But when the sky is bright,
    And all the stars are high,
My soul feels light,
    As though 't would fly.

QUEEN. Ye wailing notes! encompass earth—
        then haste
To regions dark, and bid the gates wide stand

For Rosamond the Fair.   She comes to join,
With tenor light, and vain lascivious airs,
Pale Hecate's bands, and play coquetries there.

[*Going towards the Maze.*

How awful is this silence deep!   List! list!
Some little insect buzzing by in glee,
His love-tale to his listening fair he sings.
No wandering phantom or seraphic ghost
Shall turn me from my resolution firm.
Conscience! thou busy, meddling monitor!
Trust me awhile, and I will pay arrears;
But stand aside just now, and let me lead.
We'll meet again: if not on earth—ah, where?
Don't doubt, thou Censor, I'll keep faith with thee.
Ah! must I—can I—shall I—dare I do it?
Put out that spark, which then no human skill
Could to that form restore one ray?—spoiling
Those heaving orbs that mock the mountain snow,
Tinged by Apollo's parting glance on earth,
Giving those dimples to the filthy worm,
E'en where the king has kissed?—But soft!—
            what's this? [*Walking slowly and looking around.*
Just here some ancient river calmly flows,
Sweet with the lavish vernal breeze, which oft
The flowing locks hath turned aside to kiss
The bronzéd brow of my unfaithful prince.
Must I turn vulture in his Paradise?
And with the vigour of my talons tear
From out their sockets deep those floating eyes
He doats upon?   O Night! thou kind ally,
Fold thickly over me thine ebon cloak;
My angry purpose thus conceal and aid.
'T is now this love-lorn rival I must drive
To Death's unfathomed bed.—But stay!   What
            passed?

Tush! tush! the wind sweeps roughly o'er the
    stream;
And the tall pine, as quivering marshy reed,
Makes fear a body animate with eyes,
And arms, and bony hands.—Conscience, be still!
'T is better far that I in this affair
Should take the lead. I'll make amends, I said,
And for my vengeance praise the god of hell.
Hark! hark! the voice says "Stay! stay!—list!"
      But why—why stay?
Some angel looking o'er the battlements,
Just near that silvery cloud now passing o'er—
'T is passing—passing slow—a beauteous form
Is watching me, and cries, " In mercy hold!"
I dare not stay, but onward, onward!—Hark!
I hear the watch-dog howling very low,
To urge, perhaps, some prowling gipsy's foot
To turn away from sin. 'T is Night's low voice,
And begs with trembling cry to hold me back!
Again!—again I hear some morbid fiend,
With mission from his burning home, say "Stay."
'T is vain! Hopeless, joyless, fearless, and cursed,
Sick conscience low deposed—Revenge! revenge!
Hark! list! It is some trembling voice I hear.
Hark! hark!

Song heard.

When I'm in heaven, I'll tell thy love for me,
      Most noble prince!
And o'er the battlements I'll try to see—
      Ay, e'en from thence!
And ask the angels there to dry my tears,
And wake me when my precious prince appears.

QUEEN. It is that wicked Rosamond,
Now desecrating hills and vales once more.
But soon dull silence shall ensue. Awhile,

7

Make merriment with dying moments now,
And gather scraps of life's fatuity,
And all thy miserable ends and ways,
To make a volume of hypocrisy,
As present to the company of ghosts
Who wait for thee, Fair Rosamond,
Ere they take voyage o'er the gloomy Styx!

SCENE 2.

The Labyrinth.　The QUEEN *and* ROSAMOND.

QUEEN. I come to be the messenger of peace—
Of .peace that never ends, my lady fair.
Say, shall I wile away these slow-paced hours,
Or hasten on, by magic wand of mine,
Thy bosom's lord to thine expectant arms?
　　ROS. (*looking up, and starting*). If thou art human,
　　　　or whate'er thou art,
Oh! break this awful spell, and tell me true:
Hast thou some mission terrible?　Ah! ah!
Thy pallid lip declares it.　What art thou?
Whence comest thou? Thou dreadful thing, declare!
　　QUEEN (*stamps and advances*).　The hated, hateful
　　　　Elenor, thy queen,
A vassal's victim, once a monarch's pride,
Seeks audience of the evil Rosamond!
　　　　　　　　[ROSAMOND *sinks back and swoons.*
　　QUEEN (*whispering*). 'T is heaven, or hell, that
　　　　smiles upon me now,
And this most opportune occasion grants.
The warrant for thy death, this scroll,
Dissolves the sin, and then absolves my soul.
I purchased absolution for thy blood—
(The Rose of Ditchley Maze!)—to stay its course
By burning poison or by angry force.

Rail on! rail on! ye spirits in the skies!
I hold authority from Rome. Hell cries!
  [*Taking a phial from her breast, approaches* ROSAMOND,
    and, affecting to support her, speaks in a feigned voice.

My lady fair, thy maid attends thee here.
This draught nectarean will quick revive
That light which, too far sinking, yields to death.
Thy lord will soon return to thine embrace.
                  [*Holds herself back, and puts the
                    draught to* ROSAMOND'S *mouth.*

Great lady, take—and this—and this—[*Begins to pour.*
                And this—
                  [*Continues to pour.*

How soon it takes effect! She sleeps! she sleeps!
How ghastly pale she turns! A heavy sweat
Her every dimple fills. Where's beauty now?
All fled! all fled!—in parts respective gone,
To clothe the lily and revive the rose,
And thus adorn its native settlements;
Wearing its virgin blushes there, unstained
By false affections or by mortal lusts.
    ROS. (*opening her eyes with wandering gaze*). Where is
        the cake to give this Cerberus?
    QUEEN. Has placid evening's mild restoring
        balm
Quickened thy virtue, Mistress Rosamond?
    ROS. Ah, mistress, mistress! whence proceeds
        this sound?
There, hold me!—Aba—Aba—— Save me now?
    QUEEN. Sweet Rose, thy lord is near thee now—
Bends by thy knee, and wipes thy pallid face.
    ROS. That voice is hoarse: I've heard it in my
        dreams.
    QUEEN. Thy blood flows lazily; thy lair is soft,
Good Mistress Rosamond.

Ros. "Good mistress !" Sooth I I dreamt
A dreary dream, that, 'midst of sulph'rous mists,
Some hideous thing was crouching by my side :
It sucked my breath insatiate, that awful form !

QUEEN (*aside*). Ha! ha! fastidious Mistress Rosa-
mond ! [ROSAMOND's *head falls on her breast.*
How now, my drooping posy flower, how now ?
Thy head is pendulous, as if 't were filled
With juice from Grenada, and rocks about
As stately vessel on a billow crest.

Ros. (*opening her eyes and appearing composed*). What see
I now? The queen? Art thou the queen?

QUEEN. Look not on me! I can forgive thee now,
But rather look at eve's soft golden beam :
Take thy last look of her, Fair Rosamond !
Thou see'st she blushes deeply as thou look'st.

Ros. And do thou look on the high and azure
throne,
Whence Vengeance, winged with burning wrath,
shall come.
Darest thou— defying all the laws of earth,
And all the dread magnificence of Heaven—
A foul and dastard murder perpetrate ?

QUEEN. I—I—murder! Dare—I—murder ? I ?
Ros. Yes. Would'st thou kill a hapless penitent?
QUEEN. Thine infamy now brings it on thine
head,
And I am but an humble instrument
In Heaven's avenging hand to punish thee.
This hour—triumphant hour !—is all mine own :
My joy, my long-sought joy, is now possessed.
Ah, ah ! why beat so high, thou merry heart !
Wait, flutt'rer, the consummation of our joys !

Ros. Ah, this is Death's own chilling hand I
feel

Welcome is death—·I yield—farewell to all !
> [ROSAMOND'S *body sinks falls off the seat.*

QUEEN.   Unravelled   mystery — she   bows   to
   Death !
That mystic crash !   The throne of intellect
Now falls !   What countless streams of thought
   rush forth,
As though their occupation gone !   Electric touch !
Region mysterious ! how prostrate now !
Thy secret purposes are closed : that part—
That something of eternity is gone,
As some far-distant sail ; 't was but a speck—
An atom quivering on the horizon bright—
Then sunk for ever on the viewless sea.

Ros.   All o'er, all o'er !   I do confess my sins !
Accept my prayer—forgive.   I faint, I die !

QUEEN.   Bear up awhile——
Ros.   No more ! 't is past, I die !

QUEEN.   Ha ! ha !   Fair Rosamond, thou Parian
   fair,
Tell the cold grave that I thee forward sent,
A truant mistress for cold ugly Death ;
And when in joy he gapes convulsively,
Seeking to press thee to his chapless jaws,
And mumbles o'er thy lips as if in love,
Tell him that I thy sole brideswoman was,
And sent thee in the heyday of thy sins
To his encircling, gaunt, and scaléd arms !
> [ROSAMOND *sinks in death,* ELEANORA *frantic with joy.*

She dies !   Regale thyself, thou gallant heart,
And watch awhile this waxen, wanton thing,
While every atom of mortality,
And all the careless matter, thus forlorn,
Decline and sink into eternal sleep.
All that the everlasting world awards—·

The maybe and vast mysteries to come
She may surmise at leisure, now, alone;
The petty life of Time is over now,
All gone as passing cloud dispersed for aye.
Well, now, ye fairies, trip upon the green;
Let Echo hasten hence to join the song;
Let Hate and Murder wild, with angry eye,
Take part and join this merry midnight glee.

[ROSAMOND'S body quivers.

Tut! tut! say, why this quivering, quailing, dear?
Quibbling with death? 'T is past; but now I fear
—So—so—thy bridegroom's arms thou likest not;
Thou shrink'st, and may'st distort thy comeliness;
Thy lingering beauty may remain awhile,
And breed grave doubts in grave fools' heads;
      and then
Suspicion in her jaunting car may wake.

[A dead silence.

Come, spirits, brand her as your own,
And lead her blindfold to her kindred sprites—
The land of woe and toil. You'll prove her cow-
      ard,
And truant if she can; but gripe her hard;
Entwine your web-like forms, and if she trips,
Then dash into the grave: her hopeless hope
Thus blast, and lash the vile offender home.

[Pauses.

Dark midnight, leaning on his ebon wand,
Complaining, walks with melancholy steps.
Where's Henry now? false king! Where now,
      pale "rose,"
Where is thy lord? What, moody and chagrined?
Hast thou no answer? Well, I thee will tell.
He dreams of gold and glittering scimitars,
And on thy Parian breast he vows again

"*But hark! 't is Aba now returned;*
Or is't the gusty wind moaning so low?"

Soon to recline. Fond fool! deceitful, vile!
Thy palling charms, wan nun, he 'll soon forsake.

> [*Approaching the body, she kicks the face.*

Those heaving pangs have rent and marked her
    face,
And there———   [*Leaves the Labyrinth.*

        But hark! 't is Aba now returned;
Or is 't the gusty wind moaning so low?
Or some intrusive wandering serf? Ye stars,
And placid moon, and thou, unslumbering sea,
Now bear me witness I am merciful,
And but performed the will of vengeful Heaven.

> [*Returns to the Labyrinth.*

Now here, fair dame, we part, and I must beg
Thy silence on our meeting's cause. What, still
In moods? Come, bounding, panting Fear, thy
    nod
I now obey, and leave this company
Of solemn silent things.   [*A voice is heard.*
          Rest, spirit, rest.

.

SCENE 3.

À BECKET *alone.*

À BECKET. And does a judgment day appear so
    soon
Upon the heels of sin so rapidly?
There is a whirlwind I must boldly meet,
And yet there is a haven, yea, for me,
Encircled by that Everlasting One
Who bade the storm be dumb, and walked the sea;

And then my soul, from every trammel free,
By no such tedious grades as mark on earth
Its slow development, triumphantly
Shall range the ever-endless space
Through all the ethereal heights and baseless
      depths
Of knowledge spiritual and grand,
Free from the puny power of ingrate kings.
Come, black conspiracy, I see thee now ;
My real self thou canst not reach.
O Mary! grant me patience to endure,
And as a soldier of the cross to die.
Angels of light, direct my trembling step,
While I approach the goal—the end of things.
I do not ask delay, for well I know
The true interpretation of my dreams.
I do not bow before sick royalty,
And all its earthy meek vicissitudes,
But humbly bow before the King of kings!

SCENE 4.

REGINALD FITZ-URSE, WILLIAM DE TRACEY, HUGH DE MOR-
    VILLE, *and* RICHARD BRETTS, *misunderstanding the* KING,
    and thinking to please him, determine to assassinate the ARCH-
    BISHOP *when entering Canterbury Cathedral.*

À BECKET. Gay knight, save fare thee well, no
    more.
But warn thy master now that every lance
His vaunting hand shall dare to cast, recoils,
Turning its glittering point upon himself ;

And e'en his blazing mail and all his knights,
And all the prowess of his daring soul,
Shall fall before great Rome's omnipotence.

DE TRACEY. Let's follow quickly, or we miss
our end.
See, see! he hastens to the altar steps :
All join, be firm, but hold no parley now,
Or some may wince under his rhapsody.

ARCH. Why, goodly gentlemen, what summons
now ?

FITZ-URSE. Proud priest, we come to teach thee
how to fall.
Instead of quarts of sack, thou shalt have gall.

À BECKET. Ye stand on sacred ground, I warn
ye all.
What! seek my blood ? e'en here must I now fall ?

DE T. If thou hast any prayers to say, say
now.
We've sworn to drive thy vicious soul below,
[Deals blow. All draw.
And thus obey thy injured sovereign's will.
'T will stay a base rebellious tongue awhile.

DE MORVILLE. Remember all! he wears a puis-
sant sword,
And learnt his passes well in bloody France.

À BECKET. Who willed this strange assault ?
Help! help! Avaunt,
Ye braggart knaves! myself ye cannot kill.
That villain's axe hath wearied me,—I faint!

DE T. The noble king sent this to soothe thee,
saint ! *[Strikes.*

À BECKET. Angels above, restore my strength
awhile.
And must I draw this rusty blade once more,
To punish lying lips of heretics ?

8

De T. Strike, Morville, strike!
> [*They close on the* Archbishop.

À Becket. *(draws).* Ye pirates of life's-blood!
    hold! hold, ye wolves!
Ye base-born curs! familiars of sin!
What, steal anointed breath! Heaven curses ye,
And ne'er will yield ye mercy when ye call.
> [*Struggles on steps.*

Fitz. All strike with me: release his haughty
    soul
From its incumbrances. His eyes now roll.
> [Fitz-urse *strikes.*

This heavenly lamb prefers the meads of earth,
And hesitates to seize his golden crown.
    Mor. His sins whirl round him like a fall of
    snow,
He sniffs his brimstone throne a mile below.
His breath blows out apace: let's leave him now.
Another gift from this will speed his pace, [*Strikes.*
Or some dark sprite may snatch away his Grace.
    De T. The king's own will is known to no one
    now:
I doubt if royal Henry meant this scene.
    Mor. I'll budge for absolution now, and let him
    pout,
'T is too late now to conjure up a doubt.
Farewell to England's lands—a long farewell.
Let each take bounding steps, and silently
Seek other homes and new fraternity.

SCENE 5.

An Italian Priest's *House.*

Priest. Who knocks?
Servant.   A man without asks audience.

PR. Let him come in. That murderer, I guess,
I have a rumour in my soul 't is he :
My dreams were full of him, the king, and death.
How now ?

Enter DE TRACEY, *disguised as a Yeoman.*

DE T. *(kneels and hides his face).* If absolution blots
    out darkest sins.
I would confess to thee, good father, now.

PR. What ? now ? I must go forth.

DE T.   Oh, father, stay !
I am borne down by sins which waste my heart.

PR. What sins ? of what ? Hast thou been thief,
    declare ?

DE T. Good priest, 't is true, I have been thief,
    alas !
These hands have stolen a precious thing.

PR.   But what ?
Be thrifty, man, I want no more report.
The price of every sin is small ; attend :
First pay the Church, and then restore that thing,
And then ask intercession of the saints.

DE T. My scorchéd heart will burst, dear fa-
    ther, now.   [*Throws down some gold.*
'T is absolution must be granted me :
Here 's gold—the gold—the very gold which I—
        [*Trembles very much and stammers.*
Which I received for blood—an old man's blood,
Adored, beloved by many of the good ;
His age, his office should have stayed my hand ;
But I was one of a determined band.
O priest, there is a burning heat within,
Which nought about this earth can ever quench ;
There is a tumult here of brawling fiends !
Would that the earth had gaped and swallowed me
Ere that foul sin had stained these weary hands.

PR. The holy Church hath power. Forget this
　　sin,
E'en on a king or any underling,
Whate'er his state or dignity has been.
Thou hast confessed ; thou art absolved, 't is o'er—
The price is paid, and Heaven can claim no
　　more.
The Church will bear e'en such a sin as this,
And hide it from the eye of mighty Heaven.
Be thy victim who he may, thou art forgiven :
The Pope of Rome is Heaven's vicegerent here,
And from the treasury of good men's deeds
Will grant indulgence to thy cruel soul,
Ah, yes, for ever—through all changeless scenes,
And whilst eternity, exhaustless, heaves
Its mystic form and nature yet unknown.
But thou must pray to holy Mary's form,
And lift thine eyes to saints who live in heav'n,
To mediate 'tween the Mighty One and man.
　　　　　　　　　　　　　　　[*Aside.*

Now is the instant, for my darkest thoughts
To shape themselves in form of honest speech ;
But can I trust that dark tall murderer ?
Or shall I write to Rome that even yet
I have no arm I can direct ?—direct ?
Now I will try whilst hell attunes my tongue.
　　　　　　　　[*Turning his back on* DE TRACEY.

From whom or whence thou com'st concerns me
　　　　not ;
But string thy nerves awhile, just while I speak,
And think of anything thou lov'st in life,
And know that thou shalt have e'en in thy palm
The power to satisfy thy blithest lusts,
Be what they may.　There, tell them not to me,
For I have but an office to fulfil,

And am no chapman with these ingots here :
Weighed in the fairest balances they were.

> [*Throws down several bars of gold.*

There, take them all ! they are all thine—all, all !
I want thine aid to lead a truant king—
A chambering valiant thing, Plantagenet—
To his last home in safety and alone.
Thus serve the Church, thus serve thy soul. Dost
    hear ?
Dost hear ? (*Aside*). That tenfold gloom alarms me
    now.—
Or else in purgatr'y thy soul will lie,
Whilst countless years will ever, ever roll.

    DE T. More blood ! more blood ! These hands
      do writhe in blood !

    PR. The holy Pope absolves thine evil soul.—
Dost hear ? Dost see ?

> [*Shows the gold and a written paper directing*
> *the* KING'S *death from the* POPE.

DE T.   Mine eyes are full of blood !
I now see nought but blood ! My hands are blood !

> [*Sinks down, face covered.*

    PR. Man ! fool ! I see thou 'rt mad.—Ho ! ho !
Without ! Take this foul murderer away !

    DE T. Good priest, good priest ! father, hear
      me, hear me !

    PR. Hear me ! I am confessor to that king.
'T is thine to see such royal sinners breathe in
    heav'n,
Deported by the holy Church, quite safe.
Come, come !—dost hear ? I would befriend thee,
    man.
'T is no new task for thee. The Church loves
    thee ;
Now love the Church, and leave the end to me,

De T. Anguish o'erflows my soul! Good priest,
  forbear!
My brain will burst! I will obey the Church.
 Pr. Good man! See there that shining gold—
  see there!
'T will buy thee absolution o'er and o'er!
Yea, thou may'st murder father, mother, son,
The highest Churchman and the meekest nun,
And be unscathed as blood-bought sinners are.—

    [PRIEST *gives the absolution warrant.*

There, take thy warrant for the past now gone;
But show it not—ay, not to any one.
Haste, turn those filmy eyes! The gold is here.
Think of the mirthful hours 't will purchase thee,
The long carousings undelayed by want.
'T will buy thee mailéd coat 'gainst every power
On earth, and lead thee up to heaven at last,
Where thou may'st bask on golden slopes, whilst
  time
In those bright worlds is charmed in endless sleep
By cadence of the soft inspired notes
Which echo from the lips of seraphim,
Who lead the eternal choirs. Wake, man! see, gold!
 De T. (*aside*). I see but hell, which now awaits
  my soul;
And Sin is 'tending there to dash with me
Deep down into the burning core within!
I see the Primate's form now quivering.——
How to escape? How to endure? Ah, how?
There murderers, and filthy beings there,
And some I thought I ne'er should see again,
I see their angry frowns; their shouts I hear!
My fellow-murderers will sneer on me.
 Pr. Wake up, wild man! Now for thy faithful
  love;

Or shall the Church provide thee tortures prompt,
To purge thy soul of cruel murder's stains?
Awake! Why dost thou dare to stare towards me?
That was a glance of recognition fierce;   [*Aside.*
But still restrained : 't was fear, 't was gloom, 't was
     threat.
'T is past endurance now. I 'll change mine end,
And cast him on the law's deep shoals and sands :
They 'll swallow up that wretch ; and I, intact,
Will whisper warnings to the king and lords,
That murderer's arms now yawn for royal blood.
And when they ask for evidence complete,
I 'll ask their praise to holy Mary's name,
That still they live and breathe above the grave.

   DE T. I 'll leave, and see thee in the falling eve,
For hours have sped too glib since I came here.
(I 've killed the Primate by mistake, I fear !) [*Aside.*
Oh, what a rage is in his gloating eye!
He means to end my life.—I 'll fly!

   PR. (*Stamps—three men rush in*). Drag this man down!
     Blindfold him as you go!
His hours are few, or mine are full of woe. [*Aside.*
When he 's well bound in chains, bring me report.

              [DE TRACEY *draws upon officers, and escapes*
                        with warrant and absolution.

ACT V.

SCENE I.

KING *alone before seeing the* QUEEN *after murder of* ROSAMOND.

   KING. My sad imaginings portray it all,—
The rugged murderous scene now passes me.

With mournful step it stamps upon my soul!
Those sunken eyes and that fair pallid brow;
Those once bright lashes drooping and forlorn
The stillness heaving in night's lonely hour
'Midst hideous evidence. Death's work all done.
King Death! thy many mysteries o'ermaster me,
Make my poor flesh in tremor agitate.
And she is thine!—in thy great palace rests!
Oh, take a weary man, an earthly king,
Who prays ten thousand prayers to be no more!
Oh, this is agony to be alive
With spirits many and indefinite,
Making their gibes and gutt'ral challenges—
Asking the fate of love's moralities.
All sorrow now—all dead! Yes, all is o'er
On all—o'er all—those sweet idealties,
And that great company of unseen things,
In which my wild impassioned nature lived,
All gone, as faded leaves in autumn's grave!
Farewell, once sweet tranquillity, farewell!
And all the lovely preciousness of thoughts,
With all their grand magnificence, farewell!
Go, go, adorn some noble soul which wears no stain
Of earthly passions' dye! My brain is sick!
I see no more—I hear no more! No more
Life's choice desires—its bright imaginings,
Its sweet transitions charming every sense—
Inexplicable source! inexplicable end!
Its real and its phantom exercise
All o'er—all stayed! a long farewell to all!
Oh, Jealousy! thou painted angel! thou
Hast murdered happy love (p'raps unprepared)!
Why art thou so akin to gentle love?
By what embranglement did nature act
To make thee twin to Heaven's chief excellence?

SCENE 2.

The QUEEN *comes forward.*

KING. Proud Ellen, kneel! A word before we
    part.
QUEEN. Ten thousand words of praise! — a
    novelty.
KING. My tongue cleaves to my mouth—alas !
QUEEN. Hath State emergency distracted thee?
KING. Beautiful light ! illume some better world,
And let no ray be desecrated here !
Dare I forget that foul obtruding form
Is not an arméd foe for my revenge ?
Dare I, with maniac rage, tare e'en in twain,
Into a thousand parts, that murderess' form ?
    QUEEN. Are these the courteous phrases kings
        now use,
Or have Arcadian scenes taught rank abuse ?
Poor fervid lover ! rest awhile e'en here :
Divest thyself of rude absurdities !
    KING. And so you sucked the blood of inno-
        cence !—
Uncleanly apprehensions leading on
To glut the thirst of thy green jealousy;
And with those very hands—inhuman wretch !—
The doors of youthful life were boldly closed,
And in thy guilty haste that light put out,
Which vied with brightest stars in brilliancy !
    QUEEN. There was a time I thought thy head
        was sound,
I knew thy heart had many breaches there,
Last time we met in a sequestered bower
Near Ditchley Wood, just by the lofty tower.
    KING. Hear me, and stay thy wanton tongue.

QUEEN.   I hear
Such strange and reckless sounds, all heedless
    now,
From one—bold passion's slave, enamoured slave!
Who follows swift a lord, and knows not where,
Chiding in groans along a rueful way,
Laden with lustful rheums and blind dismay.
When next I do confess I'll pray for kings:
I will not burden fading memory,
Or dare to count some virtues much awry.
And yet with humble voice dare I inquire,
Has no corrupt desire burnt in thy soul?
Has no besetting sin intruded there,
And lulled dull conscience in sad perjury?
Has no black sin inhabited thy flesh,
Lodged there to incubate, and desecrate
The gifts of generous Heaven? Once-noble king!
    KING. Hold! hold thy vicious railing. Scream
      elsewhere.
    QUEEN. Much have I loved thee, king—all need-
      less now—
All o'er—in dreariness now sunk forlorn;
The comfort of thy love all past, all o'er;
So too all thoughts of earth, or hell, or heaven.
But all my deadly wrongs are known to thee:
Long have I groaned—thou know'st all this, and
    more.
    KING. Yet thou shalt prove thy misery is to come,
Ungracious ingrate! hence! away from me!
    QUEEN. I challenge thee before the Church
      itself,
Whose absolution I long since received!
Thy favoured priest was my confessor once.
Of course thou know'st thy Primate is at rest:
Some thought it strange, some thought it even best,

Perhaps its suddenness astonished some :
But if its consummation pleases one,
Perhaps 't is well, and cannot be undone.
This rescript gives me full authority to kill ;
But some are spared in evil ways awhile,
To torture queens and spoil the royal name.
Methinks old sinners should not be severe ;
You guess my meaning : let your conscience hear.
    KING *(aside).* The gallant knights in great Nou-
        reddin's camp
Have vouched you would seduce a very fiend.
    QUEEN. You never did—angels were your chief
        sport.
Perhaps thy higher nature did debate ;
But loss of virtue was too reckless late :
The flesh is weak, and fought without that grace,
Which would impede the course of lust's wild
        race.
It had its visions not supremely good,
And heated blood came rushing on the flood.
    KING. Thy vile impertinence shall not avail,
Or check the duty of severe revenge.
    QUEEN. Fear not : I will not scold thy virtue
        here,
For all such sins bring punishment, I 'm sure ;
And for thy share prepare ! thy day is near !
Yet if thou hast no sin, I 'll not condemn ;
But if thou hast the greater share, what then ?
    KING. Thou cold and daring murderess, begone !
I now remember what the French oft said,
That I should rue sad profligacy's theft,
And turn aside, ay, loathe what then seemed sweet,
As from corruption and coarse mire, and worse.
They did not say thy feline hands sought blood,
Or that thy greed for blood was quite innate,

And that thou wert a crafty murderess,
And hated every woman's loveliness.

    QUEEN. Murders are various, some prompt,
        some slow ;
Some queens have died, and no one now knows how,
Some. poisoned, some with brittle steel expired,
Doubtless a trance, or pain which made them tired,
Unless some gloomy murderer were hired,
(And loyal men that honour have desired).
Some harlots die, and in abundance sicken ;
We need not pray for them—they go to heaven :
At all events, they make a kind of leaven :
I am not sure their sins are all forgiven.

    KING. All princes foreign shall have early note
A toothless tigress leaped upon a lamb,
And mumbled o'er a form of beauteous mould,
Breeding deep anguish through the quivering form.

    QUEEN. Enigmas and mad threats must be re-
        served.
'T is my turn now.   I 'll e'en begin to scold,
Be eloquent of sins not always told :
I would not charge each vice as some vast evil,
But peccadilloes only—very civil !
Though stolen* wives may only suit a novel,
Not always fit to point out every evil ;
Yet loss of bloom precedes demise of flowers,
And no perfection can be absolute,
When royal serpents will the air pollute.

    KING. Thou dreadful Amazon, away! from me
        away !
Go forth, thou fool, and meet thy destiny.

    QUEEN. If thou wilt have my blood, take it
        e'en now.   [*Opens her dress.*

---

   * Henry induced Eleonora to leave her husband, Louis le
Gros.—LYTTELTON.

And thou art skilled in tenderness, 't is known.
I bid wide welcome to all misery :
'T is pain to live—'t is peace and rest to die.
Strike deep as hate ! I 'll meet Love's destiny.
No woman's shriek shall wake the passer-by.

    KING. I will not ease thy miserable soul,
Nor stay the rights of conscience buried there.
Thou base undaunted foe, live on and groan,
Until thy blood-stained soul goes forth alone,
And stumbles, drunk with gore, in Hades deep.
Creep close—ay, near—thy priest's phylactery
(I know thy vow is taken—I shall die),
But ever far from me go hence away.

    QUEEN. I thought 't was blood you sought—
        not infamy.

    KING. Thy very presence poisons all around.

    QUEEN. Thy senses now are exquisitely grown,
Just as the lily of the vale you frown.
Confess your fault ; it was the fair one's treason,—
She did invite. I hope you 've learnt a lesson.
Confess to me. Be not disconsolate :
Some penitence is wise, though very late.
I think I heard some sighs—you look demure :
Now, sin no more, and venture to be pure.

    KING. Ho, ho ! without ! take this mad woman
        hence !

> [*Stands aside, as though away.* KING
> *sees* QUEEN *yet remaining.*

Not gone, vile form ! Stay—stay now : look to
    heaven,
And say the record of the dying words
Thy victim in her agony betrayed.
The privilege was thine to see and hear
Mortality's last shrift in Death's cold arms,
Her heaving moans, her sacred love's last prayer.

QUEEN. Be merciful, and with that glittering
        blade
Let forth my restless blood—release my soul :
It longs to be released, poor quailing thing.
My body long since dead—it died forlorn ;
But that great mystery within its walls,
Which the Supernal hand hath hidden there,
Now lives in scorn, penned up to madden slow ;
And in its raving fits it has done harm,
Has spoiled the musings of its perjured lord.

KING. Insulting wretch !—sad ruin ! — hence,
        away !

QUEEN. Great king, now watch a woman's pro-
        phecy :
False love must live a life of fearfulness ;
Meet days of dreariness and much distrust ;
Mistake the faithful and misjudge the just ;
And, when deceiving others, be deceived ;
Bear heavy burdens, and be ne'er relieved.
It has caused murder, and oft theft—
A constant scourge : of nature's joys bereft ;
It may go raving mad, or imbecile :
'T is renegade to love—the very devil.

KING. Thou sorceress, away ! Confess thy soul !

QUEEN. But kings' great hearts should never
        be untrue ;
They do not like their sins in full review,
They love in hiding-places oft.   You know
They cause at times the very loss of life—
Ay, when not even meant ; and not in strife,
By hands intending but impediment.
I saw a fair white rose in meekness die :
Some one had poisoned it—ay, purposely.

KING. Base hypocrite, go ! talk with raving
        winds !

QUEEN. Neglect has made some beauty pros-
     trate lie,
Just as the weary flower will change and die.
Old toads infect the air and stir the mud,
And spoil true beauty in the very bud ;
And poisonous snakes 'midst weeds seek lovely
     flowers .
(As gallant kings steal into lonely bowers) ;
E'en angry winds destroy the promised spring,
And furtive hawks oft lurk where sweet birds
     sing.
    KING. Thou beldame, leave ! and from my pre-
     sence haste
To other lands !   [*Exit.*
    QUEEN (*alone*). Alas ! foul love—foul love—foul
     jealousy !   [*Falls down—suddenly rises.*
Ye ministers of sin, forsake me not !
Alas ! I know dire scenes are waiting me !
       [*Starts back. Points to an open door. Thinks
                     she sees* ROSAMOND.
See ! see ! the pallid Rosamond stands there,
As fair and beautiful as on that eve
I cast the dire narcotic in her blood.
Oh, come again on earth ! Revive once more !
Why dost thou look so gentle on thy murderer ?
I do confess. See, see ! she fears me yet.
Ah, see those coral lips again respire ;
She pleads, is nauseate with Death's cold draught.
How weird and altered is that marble face !
Its roseate hue, all fled o'er heaven's great walls,
Awaits its consecration up on high.
She hastes away, and leaves her murd'ress here—
In blood, in darkness, and in anguish steeped !
I must go hence. Some fiend, now seize my soul !
And haste e'en down into some burning lake,

And let me hide from that pale victim there!

[*Two* Officers *stop her on leaving, and take her to prison.*

Ye ministers of law, my thanks. I go:
I ask no mercy from an unjust foe.

Scene 3.

*Music—A Cavalcade—A figure of rural beauty leading twelve
Maidens dancing before the* King. *Nobles* Arundel,
Breuse, Soully, Fitz-bernard, Vaux, *and others
assemble. The* King *talks with them whilst music plays,
but looks pale and dejected. Music ceases.*

King. I sorrow much, my lords, that I am sad
In midst of so much faithful joy; and yet
I love you much for this day's toil. I owe
Far more than I can pay—but take my thanks.

Arundel. We give thee love for love, and thanks
  for thanks,
Dear liege. We sorrow much our king is sad;
Yet in these angry wars, dire scenes for woe
Cannot escape thy tender love. Here comes
Wallenge: yes, from the field of blood.

King. Wallenge, what news to add to sorrow's
  list?

Wallenge. Oh, sire, thy noblest children now
  are gone!

King. 'T is dire distrust awaits my living soul!
But tell me all, and let my proud heart bleed.

Wall. The multitude of dead no tongue can tell.
There, limbs inured to manly toil,
To brace the bow, to rule the angry steed,
To turn aside the javelin's reckless ire,
Lie lulled, and sunk forlorn—no more to move!
There, strongest bows of largest size are seen;
Impenetrable massive shields of gold,

And osier-woven targets, lying there,
Enough to quell a world of angry fiends :
The wealth of Ormuz and of Ind was there.
'T was woe, indeed, to watch the trickling blood
Saunter o'er features once in gallant life !
Dukes, earls, and lords, with broilsome boors, were
   there ;
Where many a glistening chest has ceased to heave,
And sumptuous trappings deck those frozen forms,
And varied gems which India's land supplied,
And glittering topaz with its orient beam,
The pallid pearl, the amethyst so rare,
Bright jasper's fire and ruby's burning blush,
Cœrulean beryls and gay emerald green,
Still shine with lustre as in tournament ;
There gorgeous banners yet are gay and bright,
Helmets engraved relief, alto, and base,
And all was carrion for hungry birds.
It was the saddest scene these eyes have seen !
'T was drear to stand amidst these awful things—
But words may never dare describe such scenes.

  [Soldiers *bearing the bodies of* MONTGOMERY, MOWBRAY,
   VESEY, *and* DUKE DE BRETAGNE. *Funeral march
   playing.*

 KING. Ah ! ah ! it must be so. Bring forth our
  dead !
Their spirits watch us now and share our joy.
Give them their rightful place near to our court.
The loyal noble soldier never dies !
The crystal gates of heaven will open wide,
When these true martial spirits enter there,

  [*Pointing to* MONTGOMERY, MOWBRAY, *and* VESEY.

E'en now they stand arrayed in glory bright.
Ye gallant souls ! this day from battle rest.
Faithful have been your lives : before your shades

          10

I kneel.   Invincibles I thought you once ;
But ye have bled, in mercy to our foes.
Poor Mowbray's faded fashion beckoned me,
Whilst burning steel was flashing in our midst.
Though death hath dimmed the fire, 't is even now
Not quite extinct : the noble spirit fondly lurks,
As if reluctant yet to leave these eyes,
Whence it was wont to break in lightning's flash.
Such from their honour death cannot divide.
Pale shade ! accept thy sovereign's sacred tears :
Would that my crown, and all the laurels won
In tented field and gallant tournament
Could purchase back that valiant breath of thine !
I saw that ghastly form, Montgomery,
The light of glory circling his young brow,
E'en as a halo round Night's favourite star.
Oh ! I would give the rest of this dull life
To meet the curséd arm that rent that breast.
Oh, what a monstrous plunge broke in that mail
(A present to his sire at Wallingford) !
Thus savage valour taints the soul of man.
Thy native land will ne'er forget thy worth :
'T is public sorrow when a hero dies.
Illustrious youth, accept thy sovereign's woe.
I dared to glance on Vesey's noble form ;
Ah ! ah ! he glared ; I thought him by my side,
My best, my earliest friend !   What reckless arm
Hath murdered thee ? Why didst thou trust thy
　　　age
Among thy sovereign's foes ?   That hoary brow
Tempted some coward traitor vile to strike,
And make those gaping holes, and thus let forth
The noble spirit from that gallant breast.
His hand, now scarcely cold, dear, good old friend !
We now can only sigh, and say farewell !

'Midst seas of blood appeared Duke de Bretagne,
Sad scene of reckless tumult! all now calm!
That haughty breast that lately heaved so high!
Ah!. who can mourn thee now? The rebel prince
Will spare no sigh for one who bled for him;
Thy countrymen? ah! what to them avails
That noble thoughts which might exalt the soul,
And render life illustrious and loved,
Were once the portion of that bleeding corse?
In spite of all its daring chivalry,
That arm has found a traitor's grave at last.
That soul was once a favoured spot, on which
Delighted Heaven would shed its brightest beams.
But dark Rebellion's planet came between,
And all his glorious loyalty eclipsed;
Then left him in foul darkness base to sink.

    RANDOLPH. Ye ghosts! thy dumb appearance
             now in death
Yields sorrow to thy king, who loved thee much,
But may not mourn the dead who rest for aye!
Now here, Bretagne? Farewell!

    KING.   ,   Inglorious fate!
I would forgive thee now, if thou couldst hear!
But we shall meet in some promiscuous crowd,
When years of purgat'ry have passed away.
There are within the soul harmonious strings,
Which, howsoe'er the finger of rough Time
May rudely snap, yet holy seraphs' hands
Shall gather in again, and bid them chaunt
To choral symphonies of heavenly harps;
So, until then, we part. Pale ghost, farewell!
Once bravest of the brave, Bretagne, farewell!

Scene 4.

*Suddenly shrieks are heard: a female with dishevelled hair rushes
in before the* King, *viz.,* Duchess de Bretagne.

Duchess. 'T is here ! 't is here !   Then rumour
    has been just :
                     [Looking at the King *severely.*
Some one has stolen the body of my lord ;
His corslet and his brilliant mail of chain
Have won the favour that their lord had lost.
Whose share is this ?   At any price I 'll buy—
             [Pointing at Duke de Bretagne's *corpse,*
                  her eyes darting at the King.
Yes, king, a royal price I 'll freely give.
I know the lust for gold, with other lusts,
Have rendered royal honour much abused—
Made many wars, and spilt much honest blood.
    King.   What means this fair intruder in our
        camp ?   *[Looking at* Sir R. Glanville.
    Duchess.   Perhaps it is the portion of Sir Ralph.
If so, I 'll litigate his right—'t is mine ;
And——   *[Looking at the* King.
       Heaven forbids the mightiest here to touch
The favoured body of my murdered lord.
Before the King of king's eternal throne,
High in the archéd heavens, I 'll plead my cause.
    Wall.   It is the duchess of the brave Bretagne.
    Chichester.   Our liege, dear lady, feels thy
        sorrow much,
And freely grants, in this sad troubled hour,
Thy dearest, amplest wish ; for he thy lord
The king has deeply loved.
    Duchess.   I have no lord—
My lord is drowned in that oblivious sleep
Which nought but the archangel's voice can break,

When Death shall find his sceptre broke in twain.
Oh, reverend father, resignation teach!
Dear mangled corse, give me thy icy hand!

[*Takes the hand.*

The lustre of those orbs is ever veiled;
The fount of thy enchanting eloquence
Shall ne'er respire again until that day
When Heaven shall send its radiant messenger
To roll away the stone which wakeful guards
Shall want the power to stay.   Oh, bitter loss!
Ambitious Death! thou greedy, cruel thing!—
The beautiful, the valiant, thou seizest first—
All that the heart holds dear, the mind respects,
Leaving these pallid forms our woe to soothe.
Oh, breathless clay! once more delight mine ear
With the known accents of thy tender love!

[*Becomes frantic.*

What passed, so awful, through my hollow ear?

[*Shouts and stamps.*

Who kills the lord Bretagne—now murders me?
It is—it is his well-known voice I hear!

[*A heavy bell is heard.   Moves round the camp, stopping
her ear with idiot vacant stare.   Stares at the body.*

Hark! hark! I'll haste before the Legate's court,
And claim the sacred body of my lord.

[*The* DUCHESS DE BRETAGNE *rushes in.   Court sitting.*

I come! I come! Where—where is he? Whence
    comes that voice?
Oh, pardon me, ye gentle lords! Ye priests,
Whate'er ye are, yield up my lord!

[*Perceives the* DUKE'S *corse.*

I am the wife of that poor murdered duke!
Fie! fie upon ye, priests! Oh, angels come,
And hide me with your wings! protect me now!

And if your gentle forms fly in the air,
Hover about this charnel-house awhile,
And be my witness to the powers above.

PR. Thou shalt make ransom for thy viperous
　　　tongue.

DUCHESS. But why, alas! should I disturb that
　　　peace
With earthly sighs, that have no power to save?
Thine is a state too pure for my poor love.
Ah, cruel Death! thou 'st ta'en away my all,
And left me joyless, hopeless, and alone.
Will no one help the wretched Christabel?
　　　　　　　　　　　　[*Becomes again frantic.*
Where is the king? I seek his mighty throne;
To him I 'll plead, and ask my murdered lord.
　　　　　　　[*Walks up and down, and then stops before*
　　　　　　　　　the BISHOP OF CHICHESTER.

Father, I want to see my lord again
Before he goes into the battle-field;
I want to warn him of the rebel prince,
And those false priests who at our castle supped:
They urged my lord to turn against his king;
They said they were the Pope's commissioners.
Oh, I would fondly whisper many things
To soothe his racking brain—dost hear, pale priest?
Is this a time convenient for my lord
To list the tale of faithful messenger
Come from his castle straight? No, no!
This stormy night detains his faithful step,
So my poor jaded soul must wait awhile.

PR. Thou art too bold, proud lady, much too bold;
And thy short life may find a sudden stay.

DUCHESS. No time I ask of thee. Life's pur-
　　　poses are closed:
Too wretched and too low to fear to die,

" Where art thou now ?   Oh, whisper me as wont."

P. 79

CHICH. Lady, your lord has left this weary world,
Is now in heaven above : (*aside*) yes, he is dead.
    DUCHESS. My home is now in heaven : the duke
        is there.
    CHICH. How can we now assuage this lady's
        woe ?
    DUCHESS. Dead ! dead ! dead ! who ? The duke,
        my lord ? What, dead ?
He left his couch, while visions strange did flit
And play their antics in my sleeping mind,
Ere e'en the lid of morn had 'gan to ope.
Yes—no ! E'en now his pillow is yet warm ;
His precious breath there lies, like fragrant myrrh.
Thou art not dead : from me so rudely torn ;
Thou wouldst not die, and leave thy Christabel !
                    [*Then rises suddenly.*
My love—my duke—too urgently I cry !
I call for love, as in love's transient hours,
When first love loved, and failed in utterance.
Art thou in Death's chill world, or ta'en to heaven ?
Where art thou now ? Oh, whisper me as wont
In the dear tones gone by ; or dost thou fear
To unfold the knowledge jealous spirits own ?
Another time—and thou wilt answer me :
'T is Christabel, thy wife—another time ;
And thou wilt show thy bright regalia,
Which angels have in everlasting light,
And all the grand domain in which thou art,
And how good spirits dwell and meekly muse,
In silence pass their immortality.   [*Pauses.*
Last night I saw my duke in tides of blood,
Beating proud surges from his noble mouth.
Oh, what a dreadful thing it is to dream !—
See toppling crags of ice in avalanche,
Like rolling flames, enveloping around.   [*Pauses.*

Forgive me, Death! I would be courteous, too.
Thy dire decrees and all thy rights I know.
                    [*Grasps one of the* Priests.
I see thou hast the treasures of all time:
I come to seek what once so late was mine.
Permit me here in thy untraversed world
I'll gently step, nor once disturb the dreams
Of thy unnumbered host. Grant me this boon:
I seek the body of my murdered lord,
And am but suppliant at thy great throne.
O mighty king! just in thy vast domain
Let love's all-searching eye but peer, peer in:
I'll haste away and tell no secrets,—no,
O stately majesty!—Forgive! forgive!
But hark! I feel the trembling winds of earth
Rush o'er my brow, my burning, withering brain—
I am the Lady Christabel—Forgive!
                    [*The* DUCHESS, *wandering, approaches*
                    the BISHOP OF CHICHESTER.
Oh, father—priest, good priest, proud priest—oh,
        say,
Where is the duke? I want to warn my lord
Of those dark priests who at our castle supped.
They said they came direct from holy Rome,
To hear confession of some certain sins
Ere he went forth to sink in battle's fray.
They made him promise to desert his king—
Oh, sad!—my loyal lord betrayed his king!
                    [*Then looking at* Priests.
Ye mystic hypocrites, release my lord!
    BISHOP. Move this wild woman hence. The
        bigot raves—
One of the hirelings of base heresy.
She has been taught to whine, vociferate,
And bay the servants of the holy cross.

DUCHESS. The duke loves flowers—bring in the
    eglantine,
Raise high the drawbridge—quick!—the priests!
    the priests!
There, there! hark, hark! the stormy winds re-
    sound;
But soon my love will come—I hear his voice
Of silver note: o'er hill and vale it comes.
No! no! 'tis nought but hollow wandering winds:
                                          [*Pause.*
The golden vision of my life is gone,
And I am wronged by thee, thou 'vengeful Death.
Alas, this dreadful dream!—he sinks in blood!
No! no!—Forgive! forgive! thou sovereign Death,
    forgive!
I seek my lord—I ask your royal aid
To wage a woman's war with angry priests.
                     [*Looking towards* Bishops.
Ye sycophants, stand forth! Beware! beware!
Ye rob the patient world of loveliness.
All worlds, all ages gone, all coming time
Pronounce your doom—your everlasting doom:
Ye grin in joyfulness at woman's woe.
    CHIEF PRIEST. Remove this raving heretic from
        hence,   [*Servants remove* DUCHESS.
And lull her wilfulness in ways you know:
The business of the court has suffered much.
                   [DUCHESS *is hurried away.*
    CHICH. This sight has deeply rent the royal
        breast
With painful sympathy. Here comes the king.
How weird and haggard is that noble mien!
    KING. Sad withered garlands Triumph now
        must wear.
    PR. But where is the good Duchess de Bretagne?

BISHOP. O'er-worn and wearied, she now rests
    awhile.

KING. Ye priests, some solemn duties yet remain:
Let Love, in Sorrow's garb, attend the dead
To their last silent home.   Let all we loved
Have honour, love, and ceremonies too.
May we die deaths as honourably bright!
I sorrow, friends, to leave you in such plight.
But I must leave ye all—no more to be.

                   [HENRY *is led away.   Trumpets sound.*

Old Time has borne me long enough, he says ;
And he is censor for all worldly ways :
Permits no reasoning, or fear's delays.

                          [*Exeunt omnes.*

SCENE 5.

Interior of a Cathedral.   Enter HENRY *borne on a litter.* WALTER
    MAPES, RANDOLPH, OSTARD, GLANVILLE, GRYME, GEOFFERY
    (KING'S Son).

KING. The latter part of every journey tires ;
And on this road no sun to rally me,
No rosy tapster to incite a smile,
Whose pleasant welcome echoes in mine ear,
As oft in merry times no more to be.
Stop, bearers ! stop !   Ah, Randolph ! faithful
    friend !
Here comes the weary husk to seek a home—
A safe receptacle for royal dust.
As some worn weary galley homeward bound
From Tyre's proud land has lost all precious things,
With all the purple robes and richest spoils
Of blood and bold adventure o'er and o'er—
I come, a merchant whose adventure 's closed,
All wrecked and sunk down to the golden sands.

Is there no pandect, Randolph, for the dead,
Which strictly will prevent thy king's dry bones
To clank with mischievous abuttals rank ?

MAPES. Learned justiciary, our liege to thee
Does speak.

KING. A wholesome heart thou hast, and true :
Too full for utterance.   Well, I forgive my foes.
Another time will be when stammering tongues,
Released from bondage—ah ! another time—
Another—ah, ah, ah !   [*Slightly faints.*

MAPES.   Most mighty king,
We hear thee say, another time.

KING.   Yes, yes.
Where was I ?   I did say another time ;
But yet it boots not.—Where 's my chaplain now ?
That draught—give me to drink that freezing
            draught.

OSTARD. 'T is here, 't is here, my liege ; it will
            revive.   [KING *drinks in frantic haste.*

MAPES.   My liege,
We hope, finds comfort now.

KING.   As much, my friend,
As this cold world can grant to one who falls
So suddenly.   If Heaven me more intends,
Then Heaven that more will grant, yea, e'en to me,
And rectify the past.   God pardon those
That murder kings !   And I do execute
That wish, and pardon all who murder me. [*Pauses.*
Hark ! hark ! strange sounds are whirring round
            me now :
Perhaps it is dark Chaos' progeny,
Revelling with joy to see the approach
Of Henry—warrior king ! who e'en on death
Will look undauntedly.   I cannot blench
At what I see not.

GLAN. (*aside*).   Ah, poor king! much wrong
He hath received, which thus distracts his mind ;
Or else a better Christian never lived.

    KING. Before the altar place me : slowly step.
Here my last journey ends on earth ; and now
Another awaits me, where attendance gross
I may not bear : spirits alone my courtiers—
My courtiers there ; where king and baron bold,
And priests, by paths respective and alone, enter—
Enter.—Sigh not for me, Randolph.
His ebon majesty shall find
In me a loyal subject ; and I pray,
At meeting, to prove graceful and subdued
To meekest confidence, that in the world
To which I go, there consolations are
Unknown on earth.   This world is but a prison
Of niggard bounds ; but the chill land of Death
Has regions vast and limitless and grand,
O'er which man's spirit takes a grade, a step,
Towards the ethereal eternal life.
As when inclement Winter chills the air,
And eastern showers have swollen Eurota's tide,
Poor nature, tired then of all its shifts,
Rolls onward to and fro, yet all is o'er.
Death is but vassal, and his ghastly troops
He leads but to the confines of a land
He may not, cannot enter.   Yes, 't is there
The important change is made ; there mortals shift,
And awful immortality put on.
Yet we may riddles in that state resolve—
Perhaps a sleep of countless years may pass ;
Perhaps the mortal parts there undergo
Transmissions mystic, and arrangements dread !
(I see old leprous Sin haggling with Death
For fainting, bleeding knights from Ascalon.)

These things will make the heart-strings creak,
      Geoffery :
They say thou art not mine ; I say thou art
My son—the best beloved of all—Geoffery.
Give me thine hand. There, in thy favoured palm,
I place this envied ring. Precious it was !
It sparkles now as bright as it was wont
In court and tournament, thou faithful gem !
There, Geoffery, take the gem—wear it for me
Who loved thee much, but now must leave.
      Geoffery,
I may not stay to tell thee all I would.
Upon thy filial arm I 'll muse awhile,
As on a summer's eve the lazy serf
Sinks into wholesome rest. Yet—yet—I wish——
Hark ! hark ! I hear those soft melodious sounds ;
Their lulling replication fills the soul
And solves the frozen air to sweet accord,
Which yields the pleasing balm to Death's great
      world.   [*Sinking in the arms of* GEOFFERY.

RANDOLPH (*bowing over the* KING). Thou valiant king
     —farewell, farewell, ·farewell !
What can amend this loss ? 't is woe for love.
Dear king, awake once more.
    KING (*starts up*).   It may be so.
Yes, yes ! Rebellion stood in his dark path—
The Primate, too—how cruel 't was of him !
And so he sought my blood ? Now Death is here—
Importunate—all 's well. But now I go
Where Death's power ends, to reach that pinnacle
To which the timid, fluttering, anxious thing,
This little veering gossamer, ascends.
O Death, come forth ! ·e'en thou, thy part
Shall take : the vultures' share. 'T will soon corrupt
And fade.—Farewell ! farewell to all this world !

Sense is receding now : of sight and speech
The ways are clogged ; to hear is needless now :
E'en the twelfth hour is spent. I will not filch
A moment, while this clay obedient wears
The pallid hue of death.—I die e'en as
The panting heron dies—succumbing low,
His feathers clotted o'er in streaming blood.
Once more he casts his filmy eye above
Into the heavens, amidst the fleecy clouds,
Where oft and oft he scaled the yielding air.—
I sink no more to rise ! I faint, I die !
  MAPES.   It is the dew
Of the first morn in the eternal world.
  KING. See ! see ! through every passage now
     he creeps ;
He scents the last, high fortress.   Look, he's in !
He's in the breach ! The ramparts all are scaled.
It is the priest—the black revengeful priest !—
See where he goes !   He bears the cross before ;
He stamps upon my heart ! 'T is he ! 't is he !
Relentless ! No, 't is Death !—triumphant Death !

NOTES.

GOOD AND BAD ANGELS.

OUR readers will perceive that we believe in dreams and visions, and that good and bad angels attend on the devious path of mortality, waiting around the bed whilst sleeping hours are rolling on. Perhaps we gained this faith from Scripture ; though, we confess, we have always felt that we could leave some anxieties to some shadow of ourselves, or some protector or herald, whom we could not see, but with whom we were ever ready to make bargain and contract, as to sins and fallings-off from vows. The world may be learned in many things, and know our stature, and make nice calculations and comparisons concerning our virtue and character, talents and physical constitution ; but who can follow the fairy step, or hear the mystic voice, or see the golden halo of our good angel—or collect the Circean whisperings of our bad angel, or hear the awful, yet majestic, thundering of his trident, when he fails to win our spirits, or we refuse to drink from the intoxicating bowl he bears, in which Death lies lurking ?

We know that some will smile whilst we talk thus ; but we may remind our readers, that many of the ancient heathens (probably from tradition) entertained some such notion, that beings of a superior order were ever ministering between men and God. The Greeks termed them " demons " (knowing ones), and the Romans, " genii."

Socrates said, on the day of his death, " My demon gives me notice every morning of an evil which will befall me that day, but did not give me notice of any evil this day, therefore I cannot regard as any evil my being condemned to die." Some have said this demon was his reason ; but those who are acquainted with his sayings know that he never spoke in such obscure and ambiguous terms ; if he had meant his reason, his integrity and exactness of character would have indicated this precisely.

An ancient poet, who lived several ages before Socrates, speaks more determinately. Hesiod says—

" Millions of spiritual creatures walk the earth unseen."

Hence, it is probable, arose the tales about the exploits of their demi-gods *(minorum gentium)*, their satyrs, fauns, and nymphs of every kind, wherewith they supposed both sea and land to be filled ; these are, like the age, dark and unsatisfactory evidences, standing alone, and producing no faith or conclusions.

We have preferred to talk of good angels ; yet truth requires that we should remember those words : " We wrestle not against flesh and blood, but against principalities, against powers, against the rulers of the darkness of this world, against wicked spirits." The great poet (Milton) seems to have fully believed that each man and woman had good and bad angels.

The word *angel* appears in many parts of Scripture. The Greek word *angelos*, and the Hebrew, *melach*, are both words denoting *messenger*. The term is used very indefinitely in Scripture ; sometimes the Deity Himself, his providence, and the impersonal agents of His will--sometimes the prophets and holy men : it is also extended to the ministers and agents of the devil. The Rabbins and Fathers have written elaborately on this head ; but enough appears in the Scriptures for true knowledge.

The Jews, as well as the early Christians, seemed to have believed that good and bad angels attended every one. Rhoda says (when hearing the voice of Peter), " It is his angel."

On the term δαιμων, Schrevelius, by *Major*, gives the following significations : " A god, spirit, genius, demon ; good or bad fortune, chance ; *among the sacred writers*, an unclean spirit, a devil."

Ουδ' επιορκησω προς δαιμονος [*by a god*]—*Hom. Il.* xix. 188.

Εστι δ' ανδρι φαμεν
Εοικος αμφι δαιμονων καλα.—*Pindar, Olymp.* stroph. ii. 9.

It is becoming to a man to speak
Honourable things *of the gods.*

Hederic gives the following : " A god, a hero, a genius ; fortune, both good and bad ; in the New Testament, a devil."

τς ὁ μηδησας
μειζονα δαιμων των μακιστων
προς ση δυσδαιμονι μοιρα.—*Soph. Œdip. Rex.* 1300.

What demon (is it) that has sprung, with a violence
Greater than the greatest, to thy wretched fate ?

ιω δαιμον, ιν' εξηλλου.—*Soph. Œdip. Rex.* 1311.

O Fortune, to what hast thou tended !

τις σ' επηρε δαιμονων.—*Soph. Œdip. Rex.* 1325.

What god [demon] instigated thee ?

στυγερος δαιμων [an evil deity].—*Od.* v. 369.

κακος δαιμων [an evil deity].—*Od.* x. 64.

προς δαιμονα [against the divine power].—*Il.* xvii. 98.

συν δαιμονι [with the favour of God].—*Il.* xi. 792.

Æschylus, in the tragedy of the " Persai " (620), calls the deified Dairus δαιμων.

Φευδωνυμως σε δαιμονες Προμηθεα
καλουσιν.—*Æschyli Prome.* 85.

Prometheus,
The *gods* falsely call you the Provident.

ει τι μη δαιμων παλαιος νυν μεθεστηκε στρατω.—*Æschy. Persæ,* 154.

Unless our ancient *tutelary genius* has now passed over to the army [sometimes a *good* or *malevolent spirit*, causing the good or ill fortune of men].

λυσσωντι δ' αυτω δαιμονων δεικνυσι τις.—*Soph. Œdip. Rex.* 1158.

Some demon shows (her) to him raving.

Our readers remember innumerable authorities ; and we had intended to extend this note, having collected many and various, but we fear being tedious.